The Thin Santa Claus

By

Ellis Parker Butler

THE THIN SANTA CLAUS

Mrs. Gratz opened her eyes and looked out at the drizzle that made the Christmas morning gray. Her bed stood against the window, and it was easy for her to look out; all she had to do was to roll over and pull the shade aside. Having looked at the weather she rolled again on to the broad flat of her back and made herself comfortable for awhile, for there was no reason why she should get up until she felt like it.

"Such a Christmas!" she said goodnaturedly to herself. "I guess such weathers is bad for Santy Claus. Mebby it is because of such weathers he don't come by my house. I don't blame him. So muddy!"

She let her eyes close indolently. Not yet was she hungry enough to imagine the tempting odour of fried bacon and eggs, and she idly slipped into sleep again. She was in no hurry. She was never in a hurry. What is the use of being in a hurry when you own a good little house and have money in the bank and are a widow? What is the use of being in a hurry, anyway? Mrs. Gratz was always placid and fat, and she always had been. What is the use of having money in the bank and a good little house if you are not placid and fat? Mrs. Gratz lay on her back and slept, placidly and fatly, with her mouth open, as if she expected Santa Claus to pass by and drop a present into it. Her dreams were pleasant.

It was no disappointment to Mrs. Gratz that Santa Claus had not come to her house. She had not expected him. She did not even believe in him.

"Yes," she had told Mrs. Flannery, next door, as she handed a little parcel of toys over the fence for the little Flannerys, "once I believes in such a Santy Claus myself, yet. I make me purty good times then. But now I'm too old. I don't believe in such things. But I make purty good times, still. I have a good little house, and money in the bank"

Suddenly Mrs. Gratz closed her mouth and opened her eyes. She smelled imaginary bacon frying. She felt real hunger. She slid out of bed and began to dress herself, and she had just buttoned her red flannel petticoat around her wide waist when she heard a silence, and paused. For a full minute she stood, trying to realize what the silence meant. The English sparrows were chirping as usual and making enough noise, but through their bickerings the silence still annoyed Mrs. Gratz, and then, quite suddenly again, she knew. Her chickens were not making their usual morning racket.

"I bet you I know what it is, sure," she said, and continued to dress as placidly as before. When she went down she found that she had won the bet.

A week before two chickens had been stolen from her coop, and she had had a strong padlock put on the chicken house. Now the padlock was pried open, and the chicken house was empty, and nine hens and a rooster were gone. Mrs. Gratz stooped and entered the low gate and surveyed the vacant chicken yard placidly. If they were gone, they were gone.

"Such a Santy Claus!" she said goodnaturedly. "I don't like such a Santy Claustaking away and not bringing! Purty soon he don't have such a good name any more if he keeps up doing like this. People likes the bringing Santy Claus. I guess they don't think much of the takingaway business. He gets a bad name quick enough if he does this much."

She turned to bend her head to look into the vacant chicken house and stood still. She put out her foot and touched something her eyes had lighted upon, and the thing moved. It was a purse of worn, black leather, soaked by the drizzle, but still holding the bend that comes to men's purses when worn long in a back trouser pocket. One end of the purse was muddy and pressed deep into the soft soil where a heel had tramped on it. Mrs. Gratz bent and picked it up.

There was nine hundred dollars in bills in the purse. Mrs. Gratz stood still while she counted the bills, and as she counted her hands began to tremble, and her knees shook, and she sank on the doorsill of the chicken house and laughed until the tears rolled down her face. Occasionally she stopped to wipe her eyes, and the flood of laughter gradually died away into ripples of intermittent giggles that were like sobs after sorrow. Mrs. Gratz had no great sense of humour, but she could see the fun of finding nine hundred dollars. It was enough to make her laugh, so she laughed.

"Goodness, such a Santy Claus!" she exclaimed with a final sigh of pleasure. "Such a Christmas present from Santy Claus! No wonder he is so fat yet when he eats ten chickens in one night already. But I don't kick. I like me that Santy Claus all right. I believes in him purty good after this, I bet!"

She went at once to tell Mrs. Flannery, and Mrs. Flannery was far more excited about it than Mrs. Gratz had been. She said it was the Hand of Retribution paying back the chicken thief, and the Hand of Justice repaying Mrs. Gratz for sending toys to the little Flannerys, and Pure Luck giving Mrs. Gratz what she always got, and a number of other things.

"'Tis the luck of ye, Mrs. Gratz, ma'am," she said, "and often I do be sayin' it is the Dutch for luck, meanin' no disrespect to ye, and the fatter the luckier, as I often told me old man, rest his soul, and him so thin! And Christmas mornin' at that, ma'am, which is nothin' at all but th' judgment of hivin on th' dirty chicken thief, pickin' such a day for his thievin', when there's plenty other days in th' year for him. Keep th' money, ma'am, for 't is yours by good rights, and I knew there would some good come till ye th' minute ye handed me th' prisints for the kids. The good folks sure all gits ther reward in this world, only some don't, an' I'm only sorry mine is a pig instid of chickens, but not wishin' ye hadn't th' money yersilf, at all, but who would come to steal a pig, and them such loud squealers? And who do you suspicion it was, Mrs. Gratz, ma'am?"

"I think mebby I got me a present from Santy Claus, yes?" said Mrs. Gratz.

"And hear th' woman!" said Mrs. Flannery. "Do ye hear that now? Well, true for ye, ma'am, and stick to it, for there's no tellin' who'll be claimin' th' money, and if ever Santy Claus brought a thing to a mortal soul 't was him brought ye that. And 't was only yesterday ye was sayin' ye had no belief in him!"

"Yesterday I don't have no beliefs in him," said Mrs. Gratz. "Today I have plenty of beliefs in him. I like him plenty. I don't care if he comes every year."

"Sure not," said Mrs. Flannery, "and you with th' nine hundred dollars in yer pocket. I'd be glad of the chanst. I'd believe in him, mesilf, for four hundred and fifty."

That afternoon Mrs. Flannery, whose excitement had not abated in the least, went over to Mrs. Gratz's to spend the afternoon talking to her about the money. She felt that it was good to be that near it, at any rate, and when one can make a whole afternoon's conversation out of what Mrs. Casey said to Mrs. O'Reilly about Mrs. McNally, it is a shame to miss a chance to talk about nine hundred dollars. Mrs. Flannery was rocking violently and talking rapidly, and Mrs. Gratz was slowly moving her rocker and answering in monosyllables, when some one knocked at the door. Mrs. Gratz answered the knock.

He looked like a man who had lost nine hundred dollars, but he did not look like Santa Claus
"He looked like a man who had lost nine hundred dollars, but he did not look like Santa Claus"

Her visitor was a tall, thin man, and he had a slouch hat, which he held in his hands as he talked. He seemed nervous, and his face wore a worried lookextremely worried. He looked like a man who had lost nine hundred dollars, but he did not look like Santa Claus. He was thinner and not so jollylooking. At first Mrs. Gratz had no idea that Santa Claus was standing before her, for he did not have a sleighbell about him, and he had left his red cotton coat with the white batting trimming at home. He stood in the door playing with his hat, unable to speak. He seemed to have some delicacy about beginning.

"Well, what it is?" said Mrs. Gratz.

Her visitor pulled himself together with an effort.

"Well, ma'am, I'll tell you," he said frankly. "I'm a chicken buyer. I buy chickens. That's my businessdealin' in poultryso I came out today to buy some chickens"

"On Christmas Day?" asked Mrs. Gratz.

"Well," said the man, moving uneasily from one foot to the other, "I did come on Christmas Day, didn't I? I don't deny that, ma'am. I did come on Christmas Day. I'd like to go out and have a look at your chickens"

"It ain't so usual for buyers to come buying chickens on Christmas Day, is it?" interposed Mrs. Gratz, goodnaturedly.

"Well, no, it ain't, and that's a fact," said the man uneasily. "But I always do. The people I buy chickens for is just as apt to want to eat chicken one day as another dayand more so. Turkey on Christmas Day, and chicken the next, for a changethat's what they always tell me. So I have to buy chickens every day. I hate to, but I have to, and if I could just go out and look around your chicken yard"

It was right there that Mrs. Gratz had a suspicion that Santa Claus stood before her.

"But I don't sell such a chicken yard, yet," she said. The man wiped his forehead.

"Sure not," he said nervously. "I was goin' to say look around your chicken yard and see the chickens. I can't buy chickens without I see them, can I? Some folks might, but I can't with the kind of customers I've got. I've got mighty particular customers, and I pay extra prices so as to get the best for them, and when I go out and look around the chicken yard"

"How much you pay for such nice, big, fat chickens, mebby?" asked Mrs. Gratz.

"Well, I'll tell you," said the man. "Seven cents a pound is regular, ain't it? Well, I pay twelve. I'll give you twelve cents, and pay you right now, and take all the chickens you've got. That's my rule. But, if you want to let me go out and see the chickens first, and pick out the kind my regular customers like, I pay twenty cents a pound. But I won't pay twenty cents without I can see the chickens first."

"Sure," said Mrs. Gratz. "I wouldn't do it, too. Mebby I go out and bring in a couple such chickens for you to look at? Yes?"

"No, don't!" said the man impulsively. "Don't do it! It wouldn't be no good. I've got to see the chickens on the hoof, as I might say."

"On the hoofs?" said Mrs. Gratz. "Such poultry don't have no hoofs."

"Runnin' around," explained the visitor. "Runnin' around in the coop. I can tell if a chicken has got any disease that my trade wouldn't like, if I see it runnin' around in the coop. There's a lot in the way a chicken runs. In the way it h'ists up its leg, for instance. That's what the trade calls 'on the hoof.' So I'll just go out and have a look around the coop"

"For twenty cents a pound anybody could let buyers see their chickens on the hoof, I guess," said Mrs. Gratz.

"Now, that's the way to talk!" exclaimed the man.

"Only but I ain't got any such chickens," said Mrs. Gratz. "So it ain't of use to look how they walk. So goodbye."

"Now, say" said the man, but Mrs. Gratz closed the door in his face.

"I guess such a Santy Claus came back yet," said Mrs. Gratz when she went into the room where Mrs. Flannery was sitting. "But it ain't any use. He don't leave many more such presents."

"Th' impidince of him!" exclaimed Mrs. Flannery.

"For nine hundred dollars I could be impudent, too," said Mrs. Gratz calmly. "But I don't like such nowadays Santy Clauses, coming back all the time. Once, when I believes in Santy Clauses, they don't come back so much."

The thin Santa Claus had not gone far. He had crossed the street and stood gazing at Mrs. Gratz's door, and now he crossed again and knocked. Mrs. Gratz arose and went to the door.

"I believe he comes back once yet," she said to Mrs. Flannery, and opened the door. He had, indeed, come back.

"Now see here," he said briskly, "ain't your name Mrs. Gratz? Well, I knowed it was, and I knowed you was a widow lady, and that's why I said I was a chicken buyer. I didn't want to frighten you. But I ain't no chicken buyer."

"No?" asked Mrs. Gratz.

"No, I ain't. I just said that so I could get a look at your chicken yard. I've got to see it. What I am is chickenhouse inspector for the Ninth Ward, and the Mayor sent me up here to inspect your chicken house, and I've got to do it before I go away, or lose my job. I'll go right out now, and it'll be all over in a minute"

"I guess it ain't some use," said Mrs. Gratz. "I guess I don't keep any more chickens. They go too easy. Yesterday I have plenty, and today I haven't any."

"That's it!" said the thin Santa Claus. "That's just it! That's the way tooberchlosis bugs actquick like that. They're a bad epidemictooberchlosis bugs is. You see how they actyesterday you have chickens, and last night the tooberchlosis bugs gets at them, and this morning they've eat them all up."

"Goodness!" exclaimed Mrs. Gratz without emotion. "With the fedders and the bones, too?"

"Sure," said the thin Santa Claus. "Why, them tooberchlosis bugs is perfectly ravenous. Once they git started they eat feathers and bones and feet and alla chicken hasn't no chance at all. That's why the Mayor sent me up here. He heard all your chickens was gone, and gone quick, and he says to me, 'Tooberchlosis bugs!' That's what he says, and he says, 'You ain't doing your duty. You ain't inspected Mrs. Gratz's chicken coop. You go and do it, or you're fired, see?' He says that, and he says, 'You inspect Mrs. Gratz's coop, and you kill off them bugs before they git into her house and eat her all upbones and all.'"

"And fedders?" asked Mrs. Gratz calmly.

"No, he didn't say feathers. This ain't nothing to fool about. It's serious. So I'll go right out and have a look"

"I guess such bugs ain't been in my coop last night," said Mrs. Gratz carelessly. "I aint afraid of such bugs in winter time."

"Well, that's where you make your mistake," said the thin Santa Claus. "Winter is just the bad time for them bugs. The more a tooberchlosis bug freezes up the more dangerous it is. In summer they ain't so badthey're soft like and squash up when a chicken gits them, but in winter they freeze up hard and git brittle. Then a chicken comes along and grabs one, and it busts into a thousand pieces, and each piece turns into a new tooberchlosis bug and busts into a thousand pieces, and so on, and the chicken gits all filled full of tooberchlosis bugs before it knows it. When a chicken snaps up one tooberchlosis bug it has a million in it inside of half an hour and that chicken don't last long, and when the bugs make for the houseWhat's that on your dress there now?"

Mrs. Gratz looked at her arm indifferently.

"Nothing," she said.

"I thought mebby it was a tooberchlosis bug had got on you already," said the thin Santa Claus. "If it was you would be all eat up inside of half an hour. Them bugs is awful rapacious."

"Yes?" inquired Mrs. Gratz with interest. "Such strong bugs, too, is it not?"

"You bet they are strong" began the stranger.

"I should think so," interrupted Mrs. Gratz, "to smash up padlocks on such chicken houses. You make me afraid of such bugs. I don't dare let you go out there to get your bones and feet all eat up by them. I guess not!"

"Well, you seeyou see" said the thin Santa Claus, puzzled, and then he cheered up. "You see, I ain't afraid of them. I've been fumigated against them. Fumigated and antiskepantiskepticized. I've been vaccinated against them by the Board of Health. I'll show you the mark on my arm, if you want to see it."

"No, don't," said Mrs. Gratz. "I let you go and look in that chicken coop if you want to, but it ain't no use. There ain't nothing there."

The thin Santa Claus paused and looked at Mrs. Gratz with suspicion.

"Why? Did you find it?" he asked.

"Find what?" asked Mrs. Gratz innocently, and the thin Santa Claus sighed and walked around to the back of the house. Mrs. Gratz went with him.

As Mrs. Gratz watched the thin man search the chicken yard for tooberchlosis bugs all doubt that he was her Santa Claus left her mind. He made a most minute investigation, but he did it more as a man might search for a lost purse than as a health officer would search for germs. He even got down on his hands and knees and poked under the chicken house with a stick, and, when he had combed the chicken yard thoroughly and had looked all through the chicken house, he even searched the denuded vegetable garden in the back yard, and looked over the fence into Mrs. Flannery's yard. Evidently he was not pleased with his investigation, for he did not even say goodbye to Mrs. Gratz, but went away looking mad and cross.

When Mrs. Gratz went into her house she took her seat in her rockingchair and began rocking herself calmly and slowly.

"'T was him done it, sure," said Mrs. Flannery.

"I don't like such comeagains, much," said Mrs. Gratz placidly. "I try me to believe in such a Santy Claus, but I like not such comeagains. In Germany did not Santy Claus come back so much. I don't like a Santy Claus should be so anxious. Still I believes in him, but, if he has too many such comeagains, I don't believe in him much."

"I would be settin' th' police on him, Santy Claus or no Santy Claus," said Mrs. Flannery vindictively; "th' mean chicken thief!"

"Oh," said Mrs. Gratz easily, "I guess I don't care much should a ninehundreddollar Santy Claus steal some chickens. I ain't mad."

But she was a little provoked when another knock came at the door a few minutes later, and when, on opening it, she saw the thin Santa Claus before her again.

"So!" she said, "Santy Claus is back yet once!"

"What's that?" asked the man suspiciously.

"I say, what it is you want?" said Mrs. Gratz.

"Oh!" said the man. "Well, I ain't agoin' to fool with you no longer, Mrs. Gratz. I'm agoin' to tell you right out what I am and who I am. I'm a detective of the police, and I'm looking up a mighty bad character."

"I guess I know right where you find one," said Mrs. Gratz politely.

"Now, don't be funny," said the thin Santa Claus peevishly. "Mebby you noticed I didn't say nothing when you spoke about that padlock being busted? Mebby you noticed how careful I looked over your chicken coop, and how I looked over the fence into the next yard? Well, I won't fool you. I ain't no chickenyard inspector, and I ain't no chicken buyerthem was just my detective disguises. I'm out detecting a chicken thiefjust a plain, ordinary chicken thiefand what I come for is clues."

"Yes?" said Mrs. Gratz. "And what is it, such cloos? I haven't any clooses."

The thin Santa Claus seemed provoked.

"Now, look here!" he said. "You may think this is funny, but it isn't. I have got to catch that chicken thief or I'll lose my job, and I can't catch him unless I have some clues to catch him with. Now, didn't you have some chickens stolen last night?"

"Chickens?" asked Mrs. Gratz. "No, I didn't have chickens stolen. Such tooberchlosis bugs eat them. With fedders, too. And bones. Right off the hoofs, ain't it a pity?"

It may have been a blush of shame, but it was more like a flush of anger, that overspread the face of the thin Santa Claus. He stared hard at the placid German face of Mrs. Gratz, and decided she was too stupid to mean itthat she was not teasing him.

"You don't catch on," he said. "You see, there ain't any such things as tooberchlosis bugs. I just made that up as a sort of detective disguise. Them chickens wasn't eat by no bugs at allthey was stole. See? A chicken thief come right into the coop and stole them. Do you think any kind of a bug could pry off a padlock?"

Mrs. Gratz seemed to let this sink into her mind and to revolve there, and get to feeling at home, before she answered.

"No," she said at length, "I guess not. But Santy Claus could do it. Such a big, fat man. Sure he could do it."

"Why, you" began the thin man crossly, and then changed his tone. "There ain't no such thing as Santy Claus," he said as one might speak to a childbut even a chicken thief would not tell a child such a thing, I hope.

"No?" queried Mrs. Gratz sadly. "No Santy Claus? And I was scared of it, myself, with such tooberchlosis bugs around. He should not to have gone into such a chicken coop with so many bugs busting up all over. He had a right to have fumigated himself, once. And now he ain't. He's all eat up, on the hoof, bones, and feet and all. And such a kind man, too."

The thin Santa Claus frowned. He had half an idea that Mrs. Gratz was fooling with him, and when he spoke it was crisply.

"Now, see here," he said, "last night somebody broke into your chicken coop and stole all your chickens. I know that. And he's been stealing chickens all around this town, and all around this part of the country, too, and I know that. And this stealing has got to stop. I've got to catch that thief. And to catch him I've got to have a clue. A clue is something he has left around, or dropped, where he was stealing. Now, did that chicken thief drop any clues in your chicken yard? That's what I want to knowdid he drop any clues?"

"Mebby, if he dropped some cloos, those tooberchlosis bugs eat them up," suggested Mrs. Gratz. "They eats bones and fedders; mebby they eats cloos, too."

"Now, ain't that smart?" sneered the thin Santa Claus. "Don't you think you're funny? But I'll tell you the clue I'm looking for. Did that thief drop a pocketbook, or anything like that?"

"Oh, a pocketbook!" said Mrs. Gratz. "How much should be in such a pocketbook, mebby?"

"Nine hundred dollars," said the thin Santa Claus promptly.

"Goodness!" exclaimed Mrs. Gratz. "So much money all in one cloos! Come out to the chicken yard once; I'll help hunt for cloos, too."

The thin Santa Claus stood a minute looking doubtfully at Mrs. Gratz. Her face was large and placid and unemotional.

"Well," he said with a sigh, "it ain't much use, but I'll try it again."

When he had gone, after another close search of the chicken yard and coop, Mrs. Gratz returned to her friend, Mrs. Flannery.

"Purty soon I don't belief any more in Santy Claus at all," she said. "Purty soon I have more beliefs in chicken thiefs than in Santy Claus. Yet a while I beliefs in him, but, one more of those comeagains, and I don't."

"He'll not be comin' back any more," said Mrs. Flannery positively. "I'm wonderin' he came at all, and the jail so handy. All ye have t' do is t' call a cop."

"Sure!" said Mrs. Gratz. "But it is not nice I should put Santy Claus in jail. Such a liberal Santy Claus, too."

"Have it yer own way, ma'am," said Mrs. Flannery. "I'll own 'tis some different whin chickens is stole. 'Tis hard to expind th' affections on a bunch of chickens, but, if any one was t' steal my pig, t' jail he would go, Santy Claus or no Santy Claus. Not but what ye have a kind heart anyway, ma'am, not wantin' t' put th' poor fellow in jail whin he has already lost nine hundred dollars, which, goodness knows, ye might have t' hand back, was th' law t' take a hand in it."

"So!" said Mrs. Gratz. "Such is the law, yet? All right, I don't belief in chicken thiefs, no matter how much he comes again. I stick me to Santy Claus. Always will I belief in Santy Claus. Chicken thiefs gives, and wants to take away again, but Santy Claus is always giving and never taking."

"Ye 're fergettin' th' chickens that was took," suggested Mrs. Flannery.

"Took?" said Mrs. Gratz.

"Tooken," Mrs. Flannery corrected.

"Tooked?" said Mrs. Gratz. "I beliefs me not in Santy Claus that way. I beliefs he is a good old man. For givings I beliefs in Santy Claus, but for takings I beliefs in tooberchlosis bugs."

"An' th' busted padlock, then?" asked Mrs. Flannery.

"Ach!" exclaimed Mrs. Gratz. "Them reindeers is so frisky, yet. They have a right to kick up and bust it, mebby."

Mrs. Flannery sighed.

"'T is a grand thing t' have faith, ma'am," she said.

"Yes," said Mrs. Gratz indolently, "that's nice. And it is nice to have nine hundred dollars more in the bank, ain't it?"

THE END

The Cheerful Smugglers

By

Ellis Parker Butler

The Cheerful Smugglers

I

THE FENELBY TARIFF

Bobberts was the baby, and ever since Bobberts was bornand that was nine months next Wednesday, and just look what a big, fat boy he is now!his parents had been putting all their pennies into a little pottery pig, so that when Bobberts reached the proper age he could go to college. The money in the little pig bank was officially known as "Bobberts' Education Fund," and next to Bobberts himself was the thing in the house most talked about. It was "Tom, dear, have you put your pennies in the bank this evening?" or "I say, Laura, how about Bobberts' pennies today. Are you holding out on him?" And then, when they came to count the contents of the bank, there were only twentythree dollars and thirtyeight cents in it after nine months of faithful penny contributions.

That was how Fenelby, who had a great mind for such things, came to think of the Fenelby tariff. It was evident that the penny system could not be counted on to pile up a sum large enough to see Bobberts through Yale and leave a margin big enough for him to live on while he was getting firmly established in his profession, whatever that profession might be. What was needed in the Fenelby family was a system that would save money for Bobberts gently and easily, and that would not be easy to forget nor be too palpable a strain on the Fenelby income. Something that would make them save in spite of themselves; not a direct tax, but what you might call an indirect taxand right there was where and how the idea came to Fenelby.

"That's the idea!" he said to Mrs. Fenelby. "That is the very thing we want! An indirect tax, just as this nation pays its taxes, and the tariff is the very thing! It's as simple as A B C. The nation charges a duty on everything that comes into the country; we will charge a duty on everything that comes into the house, and the money goes into Bobberts' education fund. We won't miss the money that way. That's the beauty of an indirect tax: you don't know you are paying it. The government collects a little on one thing that is imported, and a little on another, and no one cares, because the amount is so small on each thing, and yet look at the totalhundreds of millions of dollars!"

"Goodness!" exclaimed Mrs. Fenelby. "Can we save that much for Bobberts? Of course, not hundreds of millions; but if we could save even one hundred thousand dollars"

"Laura," said Mr. Fenelby, "I don't believe you understand what I mean. If you would pay a little closer attention when I am explaining things you would understand better. A tariff doesn't make money out of nothing. How could we save a hundred thousand dollars out of my salary, when the whole salary is only twentyfive hundred dollars a year, and we spend every cent of it?"

"But, Tom dear," said Mrs. Fenelby, "how can I help spending it? You know I am just as economical as I can be. You said yourself that we couldn't live on a cent less than we are spending. You know I would be only too glad to save, if I could, and I didn't get that new dress until you just begged and begged me to get it, and"

"I know," said Mr. Fenelby, kindly. "I think you do wonders with that twentyfive hundred. I don't see how you do it; I couldn't. And that is just why I say we ought to have a domestic tariff. I don't see how we can ever save enough to send Bobberts to college unless we have some system. We spend every cent of my twentyfive hundred dollars every year, and we could never in the world take two hundred and fifty dollars out of it at one time and put it in the bank for Bobberts, could we? We never have two hundred and fifty dollars at one time. And yet two hundred and fifty dollars is only ten per cent. of my yearly salary. But if I buy a cigar for ten cents it would be no hardship for me to put a cent in the bank for Bobberts, would it? Not a bit! And if you buy an ice cream soda; it would not cramp our finances to put a cent in the bank for each soda, would it? And yet a cent is ten per cent. of a dime."

"That is very simple and very easy," said Mrs. Fenelby, "and I think it would be a very good plan. I think we ought to begin at once."

"So do I," said Mr. Fenelby. "But we don't want to begin a thing like this and then let it slip from our minds after a day or two. If the government did that the nation's revenue would all fade away. We ought to go at it in a businesslike way, just as the United States would do it. We ought to write it down, and then live up to it. Now, I'll write it down."

Mr. Fenelby went to his desk and took a seat before it. He opened the desk and pulled from beneath the pile of loose papers and tissue patterns with which it was littered the large blankbook in which Mrs. Fenelby, in one of her spurts of economical system, had once begun a record of household expendituresa bothersome business that lasted until she had to foot up the first week's figures, and then stopped. There were plenty of blank leaves in the book. Mr. Fenelby dipped his pen in the ink. Mrs. Fenelby took up her sewing, and began to stitch a seam. Bobberts lay asleep on the lounge at the other side of the room.

Mr. Fenelby was not over thirty. His chubby, smiling face radiated enthusiasm, and if he was not very tall he had a noble forehead that rounded up to meet the baldness that began so far back that his hat showed a little halfmoon of baldness at the back. He looked cheerfully at the world through rather strong spectacles, and everyone said how much he looked like Bobberts. Mrs. Fenelby was younger, but she took a much more matteroffact view of life and things, and Mr. Fenelby never ceased congratulating himself on having married her. "My wife Laura," he would say to his friends, "has great executive ability. She is a wonder. I let her attend to the little details." The truth was that she managed him, and managed the house, and managed all their affairs. She took to the management naturally and Mr. Fenelby did not know that he was being managed. They were very happy.

Mr. Fenelby turned toward his wife suddenly, still holding his pen in his hand. He had not written a word, but his face glowed.

"I tell you, Laura!" he exclaimed. "This is the best idea we have had since we were married! It is a big idea! What we ought to dowhat we will dois to have a family congress and adopt this tariff in the right way, and write it down. That is what we will doand then, any time we want to change the tariff we will have a session of the family congress, and vote on it."

"That will be nice, Tom," said Mrs. Fenelby, biting off her thread, but not looking up. Mr. Fenelby turned back to his blankbook. He dipped his pen in the ink again, and hesitated.

"How would it do," he asked, turning to Laura again, "to call it the 'United States of Fenelby?' Or the 'Commonwealth of Fenelby?' No!" he exclaimed, "I'll tell you what we will call itwe will call it the 'Commonwealth of Bobberts,' for that is what it is. 'The Domestic Tariff of the Commonwealth of Bobberts!'"

"Yes," said Mrs. Fenelby, holding up her sewing and looking at it with her head tilted to one side, "that will be nice."

Mr. Fenelby wrote it in his blankbook, at the top of the first blank page.

"Fine!" said Mr. Fenelby, growing more enthusiastic as the idea expanded in his mind. "And the congress will be composed of everyone in the family. No taxation without representation, you knowthat is the American way of doing things. Everything that comes into the house has to pay a duty, so everyone in the family has a vote, and every so often the congress will meet in the parlor here"

"Does Bobberts have a vote?" asked Mrs. Fenelby.

"Ahwell, Bobberts is hardly old enough, you know," said Mr. Fenelby hesitatingly. "We willNo," he said with sudden inspiration, "Bobberts will not have a vote. Bobberts will be a Territory! That is it. Grownups will be States and infants will be Territories. Bobberts can't vote, but he can attend the meetings of congress and he can have a voice in the debates. He can oppose any measure with his voice"

"I should think he could!" said Mrs. Fenelby.

Mr. Fenelby turned to his desk and wrote in the book a brief outline of the Constitution of the Commonwealth of Bobberts. Mrs. Fenelby creased a tuck into the little dress she was making. She did it by pinning one end of the sheer linen to her knee and then running her thumb up and down the folded tuck. Suddenly the door opened and Bridget entered with aggressive quietness. She was a plain faced Irishwoman, and the way she wore her hair, straight back from her brow, had in itself an air of constant readiness to do battle for her rights. When she was noisy her noise was a challenge, and when she was quiet her quietness was full of mute assertiveness. It was as if, when she wished to enter a room quietly, she was not content to enter it quietly and be satisfied with that, but first prepared for it by draping herself in strings of cowbells and sleighbells, and then entered on tiptoe with painful care.

"Missus Fenelby, ma'am," said Bridget, in a loud whisper, "would ye be havin' th' milkman lave wan or two quarts ov milk in th' mornin'?"

"Why, Bridget," said Mrs. Fenelby, "haven't I told you we always want two quarts?"

"Yis, ma'am," said Bridget. "An' ye can't say that ye haven't got thim iv'ry mornin', either. If ye can, an' wish t' say it, ma'am, ye may as well say it now as another toime. I may have me faults, ma'am"

"You have always attended to the milkman just as I wished," said Mrs. Fenelby, cheerfully. "Exactly as I wanted you to," she added, for Bridget still waited. "And we will continue to get two quarts a day."

"Very well, ma'am," whispered Bridget. "I was just thinkin' mebby ye had changed yer moind about how much t' git. It is all th' same t' me, Missus Fenelby, ma'am, how much ye git. I am not wan of thim that don't allow th' lady ov th' house t' change her moind if she wants to. I take no offince if she changes her moind. I am used t' sich goin's on, ma'am, an' I know my place an' don't wish t' dictate. Wan quart or two quarts or three quarts is all th' same t' me."

"Bridget," said Mrs. Fenelby, laying down her sewing, "do we need three quarts of milk?"

"No, ma'am," said Bridget.

"Well," asked Mrs. Fenelby, "are two quarts too much?"

"No, ma'am," said Bridget. "But if ye wanted t' change yer moind"

"Not at all!" said Mrs. Fenelby, kindly but firmly. "Goodnight, Bridget."

Bridget backed out of the door, and Mr. Fenelby, who had kept his head close to his book, turned to his wife with a frown on his brow.

"What is it, dear?" asked Mrs. Fenelby, after a fleeting glance at his face.

"Laura," he said, "what shall we do with Bridget?"

Mrs. Fenelby looked up quickly. She quite forgot her sewing.

"Do with Bridget?" she asked. "What do you mean, Tom? Has Bridget said anything about leaving? And I was only this afternoon congratulating myself on how good she was! I declare I don't know what this world is going to do for servantswe pay Bridget more than anyone in this town, I know we do, and treat her like one of the family, almost, and now she is going to leave! It's discouraging! When did she tell you she was going to leave?"

"Leave?" exclaimed Mr. Fenelby. "I never thought of such a thing. I was only wondering what to do with her inin the Commonwealth of Bobberts."

"Oh!" cried Mrs. Fenelby, with a sigh of profound relief. She took up her sewing again, and bent her head over it. "Is that all! Of course Bridget expects to be treated like one of the family. I told her when she came that I always treated my maids as part of the family."

"But we can't have Bridget come in and sit with us whenever we have a session of congress," said Mr. Fenelby.

"Certainly not!" said Mrs. Fenelby, very decidedly. "I wouldn't think of such a thing!"

"So she can't be a State," said Mr. Fenelby, "and if we made her a Territory it would be as bad. She could come in and talk. She would insist on talking."

"And if we did not let her," said Mrs. Fenelby, "she would leave, and I know we could never get another girl as good as Bridget."

"Now you get some idea of the hard work our forefathers had when they made the United States," said Mr. Fenelby, rising and walking up and down the room. "But of course they had no case like Bridget. Bridget is more like amore like the Philippines. Well!" he exclaimed, "it is a wonder I didn't think of that in the first place!"

"What, dear?" asked his wife.

"That Bridget is a colony," said Mr. Fenelby. "That is just what she is! She is a foreign possession, controlled by the nation, but having no voice in its affairs. She can pay taxes, but she can't vote."

He hurriedly wrote the final words of the Constitution of the Commonwealth of Bobberts in his book and drew a line underneath it, for Bobberts was showing signs of awakening. Under the line Mr. Fenelby wrote "First Session of Congress."

Bobberts awoke in a good humor, ready for his evening meal, and Mrs. Fenelby put aside her sewing and took him.

"I am glad Bobberts is awake," said Mr. Fenelby, "because now we can go ahead and vote on the tariff. I wouldn't like to do it if he was not present, because he has a right to take part in the debate, and it would not be fair to hold the first session without a full representation. Now, suppose we make the duty on all goods and things brought into the house an even ten per cent.?"

"She was busy with Bobberts" "She was busy with Bobberts"

"That would be nice," said Mrs. Fenelby, absently, for she was busy with Bobberts. "How much is ten per cent. of twentyfive hundred dollars, Tom?"

"Two hundred and fifty," said Mr. Fenelby, "and that is what we ought to save for Bobberts every year. Ten per cent. will just do it."

He had his pen ready to write it in the book, when a new difficulty came to mind.

"Laura!" he exclaimed. "Ten per cent. will not do it! What about the rent? We spend fifty dollars a month for rent, and that is nothing we bring into the house. And theater tickets, when you go to town and buy them there and use them before you come home. And my lunches. And my club dues. And your pew rent. And ice cream sodas. And all that sort of thing. We couldn't collect a cent of duty on any of those things, because we don't bring them into the house. Ten per cent. is not enough. We ought to make it at least"

He figured roughly on a sheet of paper, while the other State and the Territory attended strictly to their occupation of feeding the Territory.

"I should say, roughly speaking," said Mr. Fenelby, "that to raise two hundred and fifty dollars a year we ought to make the duty sixteen and threequarters per cent., but I don't think that is advisable. It would be too hard to figure. I might be able to do it, Laura, but if you bought a waist for one dollar and ninetyeight cents, and had to figure sixteen and threequarters per cent. on it, I don't believe you could do it."

"The idea!" said Mrs. Fenelby. "I would never think of buying a waist for one dollar and ninetyeight cents. I try to be economical, Tom, but you know you always like me to look well, and those cheap waists do not look well, and they are really dearer in the long run, because they get out of shape in a few days, and never wear well, anyway. The very cheapest waist I have bought for years was that one I got for three dollars and fortyseven cents, and I could have done much better if I had bought the goods and made it up myself."

"Ahyes," said Mr. Fenelby, hesitatingly. "I am afraid you did not just catch my meaning, Laura. It does not make any difference whether the waist costs one dollar and ninetyeight cents or twelve dollars and sixtythree cents. I mean that it would be a hard job to figure sixteen and threequarters per cent. of it. Suppose we leave the duty at ten per cent. on necessities, and make it thirty per cent. on luxuries? That ought to make it come out about two hundred and fifty dollars a year, and if it does not we can have a meeting of congress any time and raise the duty."

"That would be very nice," said Mrs. Fenelby.

So it was decided that the tariff duty on necessities was to be ten per cent., and that on luxuries it should be thirty per cent., and Mr. Fenelby wrote down in the book these facts, and the Fenelby Tariff was in effect.

II

THE BOX OF BONBONS

The financial arrangements of the Fenelbys were extremely simple. Every week Mr. Fenelby received his salary and brought every cent of it home to Laura. Out of this she handed him back a sum that was unvaryingly the same, and with this Mr. Fenelby paid his carfares, bought his evening papers, his cigars, and such other little things as a man finds necessary. It was a very small sum, and Mr. Fenelby could not have afforded the pleasures of a club, nor many other things he did afford, had he not been able to add to his purse by writing occasional bits of fiction and jokes for the lighter magazines. Some months this additional money amounted to quite a sum, and when it more than paid his expenses, he would make Laura a little present, but it was understood that this money was his, and that it was something quite outside the regular income of the family, and not to be counted on for household expenses. The result was that sometimes Mr. Fenelby had quite a sum in his pockets, and sometimes he had hard work to make his carfare money last through the week.

But one thing he never neglected was to bring home to his wife a box of bonbons every Saturday evening, and one of the things that Mrs. Fenelby flaunted before her female friends was the fact that although she had been married for five years Tom never missed the box of candy. This was the visible sign that his love had not declined, and that he still had a lover's thoughtfulness.

On the Friday after the Fenelby Tariff had been adopted, Mr. Fenelby came home with a box of cigars under his arm. It was his usual box of twentyfive, and the usual brand, for which he paid ten cents each, and after he had kissed Laura he gaily deposited twentyfive cents in Bobberts' bank. This was the first money he had put in the bank under the new tariff laws, and he took an especial pleasure in depositing it. Mrs. Fenelby had put many pennies and nickels in the bank during the week, because she had had to buy a number of things from the vegetable man, and others.

"How much did you put in, dear?" asked Mrs. Fenelby, as she heard the coin rattle down among its fellows.

"A quarter," said Mr. Fenelby, gaily. "I tell you, Laura, that boy will soon have a lot of money if it keeps coming in at that rate. A quarter here, and a quarter there! It is amazing how it mounts up."

"Yes," she answered. "But shouldn't you put in seventyfive cents, Tom? Cigars are a luxury, aren't they? And you know you said luxuries were thirty per cent."

Mr. Fenelby turned quickly.

"Nonsense!" he said. "Any man will tell you that cigars are an absolute necessity. Just as much so as food or drink or clothing. Every one knows that, Laura."

Bobberts Bobberts
"Why, Tom," said Mrs. Fenelby, "you told me, only last night, when I merely hinted that you were smoking too much, that you could quit any minute you chose, and that it had no hold on you whatever. You said you only smoked a little for the pleasure it gave you, and that there was no danger at all of its ever becoming a necessity to you. Of course, I don't care, for myself, what you put in the bank, but I should not think you would want to rob poor little Bobberts of what he really should have, just because you can twist out of it by claiming"

There were signs of tears, and Mr. Fenelby cheerfully stepped up and dropped fifty cents more into the bank. It was one of his periods of plenty, and he would have been willing to put dollars into the bank, instead of quarters, rather than have Laura think he was trying to defraud Bobberts. He explained to Laura that all he wanted to know was what he really ought to pay, and then he would pay it cheerfully. Probably all men are like that. They only want to have their taxes assessed fairly, and they will pay them joyfully. One of the prettiest sights imaginable is to see the taxpayers gleefully crowding to pay their taxes. I say imaginable, because it is one of the sights that has to be imagined.

The next evening was warm, and Bobberts was sleeping nicely, so Mrs. Fenelby walked part of the way to the station to meet Tom when he came home, and her eyes brightened when she saw the square parcel that she knew to be the box of candy, in his hand. He kissed her, right there on the street, as suburban husbands are not ashamed to do, and put the box of candy in her hand.

"And what do you think my news is?" he asked, after he had asked about Bobberts. "Brother Bill is coming to make us that visit that he has been promising for ever so long"

"Tom!" cried Laura. "And what do you think my news is? Kitty is coming to spend two weeks with us! Isn't that the jolliest thing you ever heard of? Both coming at the same time! I wonder if they"

"Well," said Tom, who generally had a pretty clear idea of what Laura meant to say next, "if they did fall in love with each other, it would not be such a bad match. Your cousin

Kitty is as nice as any girl I know, and I rather think Billy isn't such a bad sort. Anyway, they will make it pleasant for each other."

"It will brighten us up all around to have them here," said Mrs. Fenelby. "I wonder whether we ought to make them pay tariff on things. That was the first thing I thought of, when I read that Kitty meant to visit us. It does seem a little like inhospitality, to make them pay tariff."

"Not a bit!" said Tom. "They will like it. It will be a lot of fun for them, and you know it will, Laura. Would we like to be left out of anything of that kind if we were visiting any one? Of course not. I don't know Kitty as well as you do, but speaking for Billy I can say that he would be mighty hurt if we did not treat him just as we treat the rest of the family. He will think it is a jolly game."

"I am not afraid of how Kitty will take it, when I tell her it is all for the benefit of Bobberts. She will be wild about the tariff. The only thing I am afraid of is that she will go and buy things she doesn't need or want, just in order that she can put money in Bobberts' bank," said Mrs. Fenelby. "I told Bridget about the tariff today, and she was so interested! Every one I tell about it thinks it is a splendid idea, and wonders how you could think of it."

"I do think of some things that other people do not think of," said Mr. Fenelby, rather proudly; "but that is because I accustom myself to use my brains."

"But it is surprising how a little thing like this tariff counts up!" said Mrs. Fenelby. "My bills this week were fourteen dollars, and I had to put a dollar and forty cents into Bobberts' bank, and then I had to pay Bridget's month's wages today, but I didn't have to pay any tariff on that, and I had to pay the gas bill, too; but I didn't have to pay any tariff on that, thank goodness"

"Of course you have to pay tariff on the gas bill!" exclaimed Mr. Fenelby. "The gas came into the house, didn't it?"

"But you said I didn't have to pay tariff on the rent bill," argued Laura; "and the rent bill is just as much a bill as the gas bill is. You know very well, Tom, that we always figure on those three things as if they were just alikethe rent, and the gas, and Bridget,and I don't see why, if there is a tariff on gas why there should not be one on rent."

"Rent isn't a thing that comes into the house," explained Mr. Fenelby. "You can't see rent."

“You can’t see gas,” said Mrs. Fenelby.

“You can see it if it is lighted,” said Mr. Fenelby, “and you can smell it any time you want to. Gas is a real object, or thing, and we buy it, and it pays a duty.”

“Very well,” said Mrs. Fenelby. “Then I ought to pay duty on Bridget, too. She is a real thing, and we pay money for her, just as much as we do for gas, and she is a thing that comes into the house. If I don’t pay on Bridget, I don’t see why I should pay on the gas. The next thing you will be saying that Bridget is a luxury, and that I ought to pay thirty per cent. on her! Probably I ought to pay a duty on Bobberts! I don’t think it is fair that I should pay on everything. I will not pay ten per cent. on the gas bill. Everything seems to come the same day.”

“Laura!” exclaimed Mr. Fenelby, with sudden joy, “you don’t have to pay on the gas bill this month! I wonder I hadn’t thought of it. That gas bill is for gas used before the tariff was adopted! And now that you know about it, you will expect to pay next month.”

“I shall warn Bridget again about using so much in the range,” said Laura. “We shall have to economize very carefully, Tom. I can see that. The tariff is going to make our living very expensive.”

They had reached the house, and had lingered a minute on the porch, and now they went inside, for they heard the dinnerbell tinkle.

“You had better drop eight cents in the bank before you forget it,” said Mrs. Fenelby.

“Eight cents?” inquired Tom, quite at a loss to remember what he was to pay eight cents for.

“Eight cents,” repeated his wife. “For the candy. It is eighty cents a pound, isn’t it? But it is a luxury, isn’t it? That would be twentyfour cents!”

“Yes, twentyfour cents,” said Tom, smiling. “Twentyfour cents; but I don’t pay it. You pay it.”

“I pay it!” cried Mrs. Fenelby. “The idea! I didn’t buy the candy. I didn’t even ask you to buy it, Tom, although I am very glad to have it, and you are a dear to bring it to me. But you are the one to pay for it. You bought it.”

“My dear,” said Mr. Fenelby, “whoever brings a thing into the house pays the duty on it. I gave you the box of candy when we were a full block from the house, and you accepted it, and it was your property after that, and you brought it into the house, and you must pay the duty on it.”

For a moment Mrs. Fenelby was inclined to be hurt, and then she laughed.

“What is it?” her husband asked, as he seated himself at his end of the table, and unfolded his napkin.

“I’ll pay the twentyfour cents; but please don’t bring me any more candy,” she said. “I can’t afford presents. But that wasn’t what I was laughing about. I just happened to think of Will and Kitty. Will they have to pay duty on their trunks and all the things they have in them? Kitty has the most luxurious dresses, and luxuries pay thirty per cent. If she will have to pay on them perhaps I had better telegraph her to come with only a dress suitcase.”

They did not telegraph Kitty. About a week later Kitty arrived, and the next day Billy came, and to each the Fenelbys explained the Fenelby Tariff, on the way up from the station. Both thought it was a splendid idea, and agreed to uphold the tariff law and abide by it and be governed by it, and when Mrs. Fenelby handed Kitty’s baggagechecks to Tom and asked him to see that the three trunks were sent over from the city and delivered at the house, Mr. Fenelby had no idea what was in store for him.

“Mrs. Fenelby handed Kitty’s baggagechecks to Tom” “Mrs. Fenelby handed Kitty’s baggagechecks to Tom”

III

KITTY'S TRUNKS

When Mr. Fenelby went to the city in the morning he gave Kitty's trunk checks to the expressman. When he returned to his home in the evening he found Kitty and Mrs. Fenelby on the porch, and Mrs. Fenelby was explaining to her visitor, for about the tenth time, the workings of the Fenelby Domestic Tariff. She had explained to Kitty how the tariff had come to be adopted, how it was to supply an education fund for Bobberts—who was at that moment asleep in his crib, upstairs—and how every necessity brought into the house had to pay into Bobberts' bank ten per cent., and every luxury thirty per cent. Kitty was a dear, as was Mrs. Fenelby, but they were as different as cousins could well be, for while Mrs. Fenelby was the man's ideal of a gentle domestic person, Kitty was the man's ideal of a forceful, jolly girl, and as full of liveliness as a well behaved young lady could be. She was properly interested in Bobberts and admired him loudly, but in her heart she was not sorry that Mr. Fenelby's brother Will was to be a visitor at the house during her stay.

She did not show any unmaidenly curiosity in regard to Brother Will, but between doses of Bobberts and Tariff she managed to learn about all Mrs. Fenelby knew regarding Brother Will's past, present and future, including a pretty minute description of his appearance, habits and beliefs.

Brother Will had arrived that very day, and on the way up from the station the Fenelbys had explained to him all about the Domestic Tariff, and also that until a bed could be sent out from the city he would have to find a bed wherever he could, and so it happened that he went right back to the city with Mr. Fenelby, and had not met Kitty, as he preferred to sleep in the city, rather than in the hammock on the porch.

There is an admirable natural honesty in women that prevents them from claiming that their husbands are perfection. In some this is so abnormally developed that, to be on the safe side, I suppose, they will not allow that their husbands have any virtues whatever; in others the trace of this type of honesty is so slight that they will claim to every one, except their dearest friends, that their husbands are the best in the world. The normal wife first announces that her husband is as near perfect as any man can be, and then proceeds to enumerate all his imperfections, bad humors, and annoying habits, under the impression, perhaps, that she is praising him. Mrs. Fenelby had been proceeding in somewhat this way in her conversation with Kitty, under the impression that she was showing Kitty how lovely and domestically perfect was her life, but Kitty gained from it only the impression that Mrs. Fenelby had become the slave of Mr. Fenelby and Bobberts.

The more Mrs. Fenelby explained the workings of the Domestic Tariff the more positive of this did Kitty become. It was Laura who paid all the household bills, and so Laura had to pay the tariff duty on whatever came into the house; it was Laura who had to give up her weekly box of candy because if she received it she had to pay twentyfour cents duty. To Kitty the Fenelby Domestic Tariff seemed to be a scheme concocted by Mr. Fenelby to make Laura provide an education fund for Bobberts. Poor Laura was evidently being misused and did not know it. Poor Laura must be rescued, and given that womanly freedom that women are supposed to long for, even when they don't want it. Poor meek Laura needed some one to put a foot down, and Kitty felt that she had an admirable foot for that or any other purpose. She proposed to put it down.

When Mr. Fenelby entered his yard on his return from the city he stopped short, and then looked up to where the two young women were sitting on the porch.

"Hello!" he said, "What is the matter with these trunks? Wouldn't that expressman carry them upstairs? I declare, those fellows are getting too independent for comfort. Unless you hold a dollar tip out before them they won't so much as turn around. Now, I distinctly told this fellow to carry these three trunks upstairs, and I said I would make it all right with him, and here he leaves them on the lawn. I hope, dear, you were at home when he came."

"Yes, dear," said Mrs. Fenelby, "I was, and you should not blame the poor man. I am sure he tried hard enough to carry them up. He actually insisted on carrying them up whether we wanted them up or not. He was quite rude about it. He said you had told him to carry them up and that he meant to do it whether we let him or not, andand at last I had to give him a dollar to leave them down here."

"Youyou gave him a dollar not to carry these trunks upstairs!" exclaimed Mr. Fenelby. "Did you say you paid the man a dollar not to carry them upstairs?"

"I had to," said Mrs. Fenelby. "It was the only way I could prevent him from doing it. He said you told him to carry them up, and that up they must go, if he had to break down the front door to do it. I think he must have been drinking, Tom, he used such awful language, and at last he got quite maudlin about it and sat down on one of the trunks and cried, actually cried! He said that for years and years he had refused to carry trunks upstairs, and that now, just when he had joined the Salvation Army, and was trying to lead a better life, and be kind and helpful and earn an extra dollar for his family by carrying trunks upstairs when gentlemen asked him to, I had to step in and refuse to let him carry trunks upstairs, and that this was the sort of thing that discouraged a poor man who was trying to make up for his past errors. So I gave him a dollar to leave them down here.”

Mr. Fenelby looked at the three big trunks ruefully, and shook his head at them.

“Well,” he said, “I suppose it is all right, Laura, but I can’t see why you wouldn’t let him take them up. You know I don’t enjoy that kind of work, and that I don’t think it is good for me.”

“Kitty didn’t want them taken up,” said Mrs. Fenelby, gently. “Sheshe wanted them left down here.”

“Down here?” asked Mr. Fenelby, as if dazed. “Down here on the grass?”

“Yes,” said Kitty, lightly. “It was my idea. Laura had nothing to do with it at all. I thought it would be nice to have the trunks down here on the lawn. Everywhere I visit they always take my trunks up to my room, and it gets so tiresome always having the same thing happen, so I thought that this time I would have a variety and leave my trunks on the lawn. I never in my life left my trunks on a front lawn, and I wanted to see how it would be. You don’t think they will hurt the grass do you, Mr. Fenelby?”

Kitty asked this with such an air of sincerity that Mr. Fenelby seated himself on one of the trunks and looked up at her anxiously. He could not recall that he had ever heard of any weakness of mind in Kitty or in her family, but he could not doubt his ears.

“Butbut” he said, “but you don’t mean to leave them here, do you?”

Kitty smiled down at him reassuringly.

“Of course, if it is going to harm the grass at all, Mr. Fenelby, I sha’n’t think of it,” she said. “I know that sometimes when a board or anything lies on the grass a long time the grass under the board gets all white, and if the trunks are going to make white spots on your lawn, I’ll have them removed, but I thought that if we moved the trunks around to different places every day it would avoid that. But you know more about that than I do. Do you think they will make white places on the lawn, Mr. Fenelby?”

“I don’t know,” he said, abstractedly. “I mean, yes, of course they will. But they will get rained on. You don’t want your trunks rained on, you know. Trunks aren’t meant to be rained on. It isn’t good for them.” A thought came to him suddenly. “You and Laura haven’t quarreled, have you?” he asked, for he thought that perhaps that was why Kitty would not have her trunks carried up.

"Indeed not!" cried Kitty, putting her arm affectionately around Laura's waist.

"II thought perhaps you had," faltered Mr. Fenelby. "I thoughtthat is to sayI was afraid perhaps you were going away again. I thought you were going to make us a good, long visit"

"Indeed I am," said Kitty, cheerfully. "I am going to stay weeks, and weeks, and weeks. I am going to stay until you are all tired to death of me, and beg me to begone."

"That is good," said Mr. Fenelby, with an attempt at pleasure. "But don't you think, since you are going to do what we want you to do, and stay for weeks, and weeks, and weeks, that you had better let your trunks be taken up to your room? OrI'll tell you what we'll do! Suppose we just take the trunks into the lower hall?"

He felt pretty certainly, now, that Kitty must have had a little touch of, say, sunstroke, or something of that kind, and he went on in a gently argumentative tone.

"Just into the lower hall," he said. "That would be different from having them in your room, and it would save my grass. I worked hard to get this lawn looking as it does now, Kitty, and I cannot deny that big trunks like these will not do it any good. Let us say we will put the trunks in the lower hall. Then they will be safe, too. No one can steal them there. A front lawn is a rather conspicuous place for trunks. And what will the neighbors say, too, if we leave the trunks on the lawn? Why shouldn't we put the trunks in the lower hall?"

"Well," said Kitty, "I can't afford it, that is why. Really, Mr. Fenelby, I can't afford to have those three trunks brought into the house."

"And yet," said Mr. Fenelby, with just the slightest hint of impatience, "you girls could afford to give the man a dollar not to take them in! That is woman's logic!"

"Oh! a dollar!" said Kitty. "If it was only a matter of a dollar! I hope you don't think, Mr. Fenelby, that I travel with only ten dollars' worth of baggage! No, indeed! I simply cannot afford to pay ten per cent. duty on what is in those trunks, and so I prefer to let them remain on the lawn. I wrote Laura that I expected to be treated as one of the family while I was visiting her, and if the Domestic Tariff is part of the way the family is treated I certainly expect to live up to it. Now, don't blame Laura, for she was not only willing to have the trunks come in without paying duty, but insisted that they should."

Mr. Fenelby looked very grave. He was in a perplexing situation. He certainly did not wish to appear inhospitable, and yet Laura had had no right to say that the trunks could enter the house duty free. The only way such an unusual alteration in the Domestic Tariff could be made was by act of the Family Congress, and he very well knew that if once the matter of revising the tariff was taken up it was beyond the ken of man where it would end. He preferred to stand pat on the tariff as it had been originally adopted.

"I told her," said Kitty, "that she had no right to throw off the duty on my trunks, at all, and that I wouldn't have it, and I didn't."

"Well, Tom," said Mrs. Fenelby, "you know perfectly well that we can't leave those trunks out on the lawn. It would not only be absolutely foolish to do that, but cruel to Kitty. A girl simply can't visit away from home without trunks, and it is absolutely necessary that Kitty should have her trunks."

"'Necessities, ten per cent.,'" quoted Kitty.

"But, my dear," said Mr. Fenelby, softly, "we really can't break all our household rules just because Kitty has brought three trunks, can we? Kitty does not expect us to do that, and I think she looks at it in a very rational manner. I like the spirit she has evinced."

"Very well, then," said Mrs. Fenelby, "you must find some way to take care of those trunks, for we cannot leave them on the lawn."

"Why can't we take them to some neighbor's house?" asked Kitty. "I am sure some neighbor would be glad to store them for me for awhile. Aren't you on good terms with your neighbors, Laura?"

"The Rankins might take them," said Laura, thoughtfully. "They have that vacant room, you know, Tom. They might not mind letting us put them in there."

"I don't know the Rankins," said Kitty, "but I am sure they are perfectly lovely people, and that they would not mind in the least."

"I know they wouldn't," said Mr. Fenelby. "Rankin would be glad to do something of that sort to repay me for the number of times he has borrowed my lawnmower. I will step over after dinner and ask him."

"Are you sure, very sure, that you do not mind, Kitty?" asked Mrs. Fenelby. "You will not feel hurt, or anything?"

"Oh, no!" said Kitty, lightly. "It will be a lark. I never in my life went visiting with three trunks, and then had them stored in another house. It will be quite like being shipwrecked on a desert island, to get along with one shirtwaist and one handkerchief."

"It will not be quite that bad, you know," said Mr. Fenelby, with the air of a man stating a great discovery, "because, don't you see, you can open your trunks at the Rankins', and bring over just as many things as you think you can afford to pay on."

For some reason that Mr. Fenelby could not fathom Kitty laughed merrily at this, and then they all went in to dinner. It was a very good dinner, of the kind that Bridget could prepare when she was in the humor, and they sat rather longer over it than usual, and then Mr. Fenelby proposed that he should step over to the Rankins' and arrange about the storage of Kitty's trunks, and on thinking it over he decided that he had better step down to the station and see if he could not get a man to carry the trunks across the street and up the Rankins' stairs. As they filed out of the house upon the porch, Kitty suddenly decided that it was a beautiful evening for a little walk, and that nothing would please her so much as to walk to the station with Mr. Fenelby, if Laura would be one of the party, and after running up to see that Bobberts was all right, Laura said that she would go, and they started. As they were crossing the street to the Rankins' Kitty suddenly turned back.

"Never in the history of trunks was the act of
unpacking done so quickly or so recklessly" "Never in the history of trunks was the act of
unpacking done so quickly or so recklessly"
"You two go ahead," she said. "The air will do you good, Laura. I have something I want to do," and she ran back.

She entered the house, and looked out of the window until she saw the Fenelbys go into the Rankins' and come out again, and saw them start to the station, but as soon as they were out of sight she dashed down the porch steps and threw open the lids of her trunks. Never in the history of trunks was the act of unpacking done so quickly or so recklessly. She dived into the masses of fluffiness and emerged with great armfuls, and hurried them into the house, up the stairs, and into her closet, and was down again for another load. If she had been looting the trunks she could not have worked more hurriedly, or more energetically, and when the last armful had been carried up she slammed the lids and turned the keys, and sank in a graceful position on the lower porch step.

Mr. and Mrs. Fenelby returned with leisurely slowness of pace, the station loafer and manoflittlework slouching along at a respectful distance behind them. Kitty greeted them with a cheerful frankness of face. The manoflittlework looked at the three big trunks as if their size was in some way a personal insult to him. He tried to assume the look of a man who had been cozened away from his needed rest on false pretences.

"I didn't know as the trunks was as big as them," he drawled. "If I'd knowed they was, I wouldn't of walked all the way over here. Fifty cents ain't no fair price for carryin' three trunks, the size and heft of them, acrosswell, say this is a sixty foot streetsay, eighty feet, and up a flight of stairs. I don't say nothin', but I'll leave it to the ladies."

"Fifty cents!" cried Kitty. "I should think not! Why, I didn't imagine you would do it for less than a dollar. I mean to pay you a dollar."

"That's right," said the man. "You see I have to walk all the way back to the station when I git through, too. My time goin' and comin' is worth something."

"With all the grace of a Sandow" "With all the grace of a Sandow"
He bent down and took the largest trunk by one handle, to heave it to his back, and as he touched the handle the trunk almost arose into the air of its own accord. The man straightened up and looked at it, and a strange look passed across his face, but he closed his mouth and said nothing.

"Would you like a lift?" asked Mr. Fenelby.

"No," said the man shortly. "I know how to handle trunks, I do," and it certainly seemed that he did, for he swung it to his back with all the grace of a Sandow, and started off with it. Mr. Fenelby looked at him with surprise.

"Now, isn't that one of the oddities of nature?" said Mr. Fenelby. "That fellow looks as if he had no strength at all, and see how he carries off that trunk as if there was not a thing in it. I suppose it is a knack he has. Now, see how hard it is for me merely to lift one end of this smallest one."

But before he could touch it Kitty had grasped him by the arm.

"Oh, don't try it!" she cried. "Please don't! You might hurt your back."

IV

BILLY

A few minutes before noon the next day Billy Fenelby dropped into Mr. Fenelby's office in the city and the two men went out to lunch together. It would be hard to imagine two brothers more unlike than Thomas and William Fenelby, for if Thomas Fenelby was inclined to be small in stature and precise in his manner, William was all that his nickname of Billy implied, and was not so many years out of his college football eleven, where he had won a place because of his size and strength. Billy Fenelby, after having been heroized by innumerable girls during his college years, had become definitely a man's man, and was in the habit of saying that his girlygirl days were over, and that he would walk around a block any day to escape meeting a girl. He was not afraid of girls, and he did not hate them, but he simply held that they were not worth while. The truth was that he had been so petted and worshiped by them as a star football player that the attention they paid him, as an ordinary young man not unlike many other young men out of college, seemed tame by comparison. No doubt he had come to believe, during his college days, that the only interesting thing a girl could do was to admire a man heartily, and in the manner that only football players and matinee idols are admired, so that now, when he had no particular claim to admiration, girls had become, so far as he was concerned, useless affairs.

"Now, about this girlperson that you have over at your house," he said to his brother, when they were seated at their lunch, "what about her?"

"About her?" asked Mr. Fenelby. "How do you mean?"

"What about her?" repeated Billy. "You know how I feel about the girlbusiness. I suppose she is going to stay awhile?"

"Kitty? I think so. We want her to. But you needn't bother about Kitty. She won't bother you a bit. She's the right sort, Billy. Not like Laura, of course, for I don't believe there is another woman anywhere just like Laura, but Kitty is not the ordinary flighty girl. You should hear her appreciate Bobberts. She saw his good points, and remarked about them, at once, and the way she has caught the spirit of the Domestic Tariff that I was telling you about is fine! Most girls would have hemmed and hawed about it, but she didn't! No, sir! She just saw what a fine idea it was, and when she saw that she couldn't afford to have her three trunks brought into the house she proposed that she leave them at a neighbor's. Did not make a single complaint. Don't worry about Kitty."

"That is all right about the tariff," said Billy. "I can't say I think much of that tariff idea myself, but so long as it is the family custom a guest couldn't do any less than live up to it. But I don't like the idea of having to spend a number of weeks in the same house with any girl. They are all bores, Tom, and I know it. A man can't have any comfort when there is a girl in the house. And between you and me that Kitty girl looks like the kind that is sure to be always right at a fellow's side. I was wondering if Laura would think it was all right if I stayed in town here?"

"No, she wouldn't," said Tom shortly. "She would be offended, and so would I. If you are going to let some nonsense about girls being a bore,which is all foolishnesskeep you away from the house, you had betterWhy," he added, "it is an insult to usto Laura and mejust as if you said right out that the company we choose to ask to our home was not good enough for you to associate with. If you think our house is going to bore you"

"Now, look here, old man," said Billy, "I don't mean that at all, and you know I don't. I simply don't like girls, and that is all there is to it. But I'll come. I'll have my trunk sent over andSay, do I have to pay duty on what I have in my trunk?"

"Certainly," said Mr. Fenelby. "That is, of course, if you want to enter into the spirit of the thing. It is only ten per cent., you know, and it all goes into Bobberts' education fund."

Billy sat in silent thought awhile.

"I wonder," he said at length, "how it would do if I just put a few things into my suitcaseenough to last me a few days at a timeand left my trunk over here. I don't need everything I brought in that trunk. I was perfectly reckless about putting things in that trunk. I put into that trunk nearly everything I own in this world, just because the trunk was so big that it would hold everything, and it seemed a pity to bring a big trunk like that with nothing in it but air. Now, I could take my suitcase and put into it the things I will really need"

"Certainly," said Mr. Fenelby. "You can do that if you want to, and it would be perfectly fair to Bobberts. All Bobberts asks is to be paid a duty on what enters the house. He don't say what shall be brought in, or what shall not. Personally, Billy, I would call the duty off, so far as you are concerned, but I don't think Laura would like it. We started this thing fair, and we are all living up to it. Laura made Kitty live up to it and you can see it would not be right for me to make an exception in your case just because you happen to be my brother."

"No," agreed Billy, "it wouldn't. I don't ask it. I will play the game and I will play it fair. All I ask is: If I bring a suitcase, do I have to pay on the case? Because if I do, I won't bring it. I can wrap all I need in a piece of paper, and save the duty on the suitcase. I believe in playing fair, Tom, but that is no reason why I should be extravagant."

"I think," said Tom, doubtfully, "suitcases should come in free. Of course, if it was a brand new suitcase it would have to pay duty, but an old oneone that has been usedis different. It is like wrappingpaper. The duty is assessed on what the package contains and not on the package itself. If it is not a new suitcase you will not have to pay duty on it."

"Then my suitcase will go in free," said Billy. "It is one of the first crop of suitcases that was raised in this country, and I value it more as a relic than as a suitcase. I carry it more as a souvenir than as a suitcase."

"Souvenirs are different," said Mr. Fenelby. "Souvenirs are classed as luxuries, and pay thirty per cent. If you consider it a souvenir it pays duty."

"I will consider it a suitcase," said Billy promptly. "I will consider it a poor old, wornout suitcase."

"I think that would be better," agreed Mr. Fenelby. "But we will have to wait and see what Laura considers it."

As on the previous evening the ladies were on the porch, enjoying the evening air, when Mr. Fenelby reached home, with Billy in tow, and Billy greeted them as if he had never wished anything better than to meet Miss Kitty.

"Where is this custom house Tom has been telling me about?" he asked, as soon as the hand shaking was over. "I want to have my baggage examined. I have dutiable goods to declare. Who is the inspector?"

"'I declare one collar'" "'I declare one collar'"

"Laura is," said Kitty. "She is the slave of the grinding system that fosters monopoly and treads under heel the poor people."

"All right," said Billy, "I declare one collar. I wish to bring one collar into the bosom of this family. I have in this suitcase one collar. I never travel without one extra collar. It is the twoforaquarter kind, with a name like a sleeping car, and it has been laundered twice, which brings it to the verge of ruin. How much do I have to pay on the one collar?"

"Collars are a necessity," said Mrs. Fenelby, "and they pay ten per"

"What a notion!" exclaimed Kitty. "Collars are not a necessity. Collars are an actual luxury, especially in warm weather. Many very worthy men never wear a collar at all, and would not think of wearing one in hot weather. They are like jewelry oror something of that sort. Collars certainly pay thirty per cent."

"I reserve the right to appeal," said Billy. "Those are the words of an unjust judge. But how much do I take off the value of the collar because two thirds of its life has been laundered away? How much is one third of twelve and a half?"

"Now, that is pure nonsense," Kitty said, "and I sha'n't let poor, dear little Bobberts be robbed in any such way. That collar cost twelve and a half cents, and it has had two and a half cents spent on it twice, so it is now a seventeen and a half cent collar, and thirty per cent. of that isis"

"Oh, if you are going to rob me!" exclaimed Billy. "I don't care. I can get along without a collar. I will bring out a sweater tomorrow."

"Sweaters pay only ten per cent.," said Kitty sweetly. "What else have you in your suitcase?"

"Air," said Billy. "Nothing but air. I didn't think I could afford to bring anything else, and I will leave the collar out here. I open the caseI take out the collarI place it gently on the porch railingand I take the empty suitcase into the house. I pay no duty at all, and that is what you get for being so grasping."

Mr. Fenelby shook his head.

"You can't do that, Billy," he said. "That puts the suitcase in another class. It isn't a package for holding anything now, and it isn't a necessitybecause you can't need an empty suitcaseso it doesn't go in at ten per cent., so it must be a luxury, and it pays thirty per cent."

"That suitcase," said Billy, looking at it with a calculating eye, "is not worth thirty per cent. of what it is worth. It is worthless, and I wouldn't give ten per cent. of nothing for it. It stays outside. So I pay nothing. I go in free. Unless I have to pay on myself."

“You don’t have to,” said Kitty, “although I suppose Laura and Tom think you are a luxury.”

“Don’t you think I am one?” asked Billy.

“No, I don’t,” said Kitty frankly, “and when you know me better, you will not ask such a foolish question. Where ever I am, there a young man is a necessity.”

V

THE PINK SHIRTWAIST

The morning after Billy Fenelby's arrival at the Fenelby home he awakened unusually early, as one is apt to awaken in a strange bed, and he lay awhile thinking over the events of the previous evening. He was more than ever convinced that Kitty was not the kind of girl he liked. He felt that she had made a barefaced effort to flirt with him the evening before, and that she was just the kind of a girl that was apt to be troublesome to a bachelor. She was the kind of a girl that would demand a great deal of attention and expect it as a natural right, and then, when she received it, make the man feel that he had been attentive in quite another way, and that the only fair thing would be to propose. And he felt that she was the kind of girl that no man could propose to with any confidence whatever. She would be just as likely to accept him as not, and having accepted him, she would be just as likely to expect him to marry her as not. He felt that he was in a very ticklish situation. He saw that Kitty was the sort of girl that would take any air of rude indifference he might assume to be a challenge, and any comely polite attention to be serious love making. He saw that the only safe thing for him to do would be to run away, but, since he had seen Kitty, that was the last thing in the world that he would have thought of doing. He decided that he would constitute her bright eyes and red lips to be a mental warning sign reading "Danger" in large letters, and that whenever he saw them he would be as wary as a rabbit and yet as brave as a lion.

He next felt a sincere regret that he had refused to pay the duty on the clean collar he had brought with him, and that he had left on the railing of the porch. He got out of bed and looked at the collar he had worn the day before, and frowned at it as he saw that it was not quite immaculate. Then he listened closely for any sound in the house that would tell him Mr. or Mrs. Fenelby were up. He heard nothing. He hastily slipped on his clothes, and tiptoed out of the room and down the stairs. This tariff for revenue only was well enough for Thomas and Laura, and assessing a duty of ten per cent. on everything that came into the house (and thirty per cent. on luxuries) might fill up Bobberts' bank, and provide that baby with an education fund, but it was an injustice to bachelor uncles when there was an unmarried girl in the house. If this Kitty girl was willing to so forget what was due to a young man as to appear in one dress the whole time of her stay, that was her lookout, but for his part he did not intend to lower his dignity by going down to breakfast in a soiled collar. If creeping down to the porch in his stockings, and bringing in that collar surreptitiously, was smuggling, then

Billy stopped short at the screen door. From there he could see the spot on the railing where he had put the collar, and the collar was not there! No doubt it had fallen to the lawn. He opened the screen door carefully and stepped outside. The early morning air was cool and sweet, and an ineffable quiet rested on the suburb. He tiptoed gently across the porch and down the porch steps, and hobbled carefully across the painful pebble walk and stepped upon the lawn. There was dew on the lawn. The lawn was soaked and saturated and steeped in dew. It bathed his feet in chilliness, as if he had stepped into a pail of ice water, and the vines that clambered up the porchside were dewy too. As he kneeled on the grass and pawed among the vines, seeking the missing collar, the vines showered down the crystal drops upon him, and soaked his sleeves, and added a finishing touch of ruin to the collar he was wearing. The other collar was not there! It was not among the vines, it was not on the lawn, it was not on the porch, and soaked in socks and sleeves he retreated. He paused a minute on the porch to glance thoughtfully at the moist footprints his feet left on the boards, and wondered if they would be dry before Tom or Laura came down. At any rate there was no help for it now, and he went up the stairs again.

The most uncomfortable small discomfort is wet socks, whether they come from a small hole in the bottom of a shoe or from walking on a lawn in the early morning, and Billy wiggled his toes as he slowly and carefully climbed the stairs. As he turned the last turn at the top he stopped short and blushed. Kitty was standing there awaiting him, a smile on her face and his other collar in her hand. She laid her finger on her lip, and tapped it there to command silence, and raised her brows at him, to let him know that she knew where he had been and why.

"I thought you would want it," she said in the faintest whisper, "so I smuggled it in last night. I had no idea you would stoop to such a thing, butbut I felt so sorry for you, without a collar."

"Thanks!" whispered Billy. It was a masterpiece of whispering, that word. It was a gruff whisper, warding off familiarity, and yet it was a grateful whisper, as a whisper should be to thank a pretty girl for a favor done, but still it was a scoffing whisper, with a tinge of resentfulness, but resentfulness tempered by courtesy. Underlying all this was a flavor of independence, but not such crude independence that it killed the delicate tone that implied that the hearer of the whisper was a very pretty girl, and that that fact was granted even while her interference in the whisperer's affairs was misliked, and her suspicions of dishonest acts on his part considered uncalled for. If he did not quite succeed in getting all this crowded into the one word it was doubtless because his feet were so wet and uncomfortable. Billy was rather conscious that he had not quite succeeded, and he would have tried again, adding this time an inflection to mean that he well understood that her object was to get him into a quasi conspiracy and thus draw him irrevocably into confidential relations of misdemeanor from which he could not escape, but that he refused to be so drawnI say he would have repeated the word, but a sound in one of the bedrooms close at hand sent them both tiptoeing to their rooms.

They had hardly reached safety when the door of Mr. Fenelby's room opened and Mr. Fenelby stole out quietly, stole as quietly down the stairs and out upon the porch. He looked at the railing where Billy had left the collar, and then he peered over the railing, and as silently stole up the stairs again. He paused at Billy's door and tapped on it. Billy opened it a mere hint of a crack.

"What is it?" he whispered.

"That collar," whispered Mr. Fenelby. "I thought about it all night, and I didn't think it right that you should be made to do without it. I just went down, to get it, but it isn't there."

"Never mind," whispered Billy. "Don't worry, old man. I will wear the one I have."

Mr. Fenelby hesitated.

"Of course," he whispered, "you won'tThat is to say, you needn't tell Laura I went down"

"Certainly not," whispered Billy. "It was awfully kind of you to think of it. But I'll make this one do."

Mr. Fenelby waited at the door a moment longer as if he had something more to say, but Billy had closed the door, and he went back to his room.

It was with relief that Bridget heard the door close behind Mr. Fenelby. She had been standing on the little landing of the backstairs, where he had almost caught her as she was coming up. If she had been one step higher he would have seen her head. Usually she would not have minded this, for she had a perfect right to be on the backstairs in the early morning, but this time she felt that it was her duty to remain undiscovered. Now that Mr. Fenelby was gone she softly stepped to Billy's door and knocked lightly.

"Misther Billy, sor, are ye there?" she whispered. Billy opened the door a crack and looked out.

"Mornin' to ye," she said in a hoarse whisper. "I'm sorry t' disthurb ye, but Missus Fenelby axed me t' bring up th' collar ye left on th' porrch railin', an' t' let no wan know I done it, an' I just wanted t' let ye know th' reason I have not brung it up is because belike someone else has brang it already, for it is gone."

"Thank you, Bridget," whispered Billy. "It doesn't matter."

She turned away, but when he had closed the door she paused, and after hesitating a moment she tapped on his door again. He opened it.

"I have put me foot in it," she said, "like I always do. W'u'd ye be so good as t' fergit I mentioned th' name of Missus Fenelby, that's a dear man? I raymimber now I was not t' mention it t' ye."

"Certainly, Bridget," said Billy, and he closed the door and went again to the window, where he was turning his socks over and over in the streak of sunlight that warmed a part of the window sill.

It took the socks a little longer to dry than he had thought it would, and they were still damp enough to make his feet feel anything but comfortable when he heard the breakfast bell tinkle faintly. He hurried the rest of his toilet and went down the stairs, assuming as he went the air of unsuspected innocence that is the inborn right of every man who knows he has done wrong. The bodily Billy was more conscious of the discomfort of his feet, but the mental Billy was all collar. He had never known a collar to be so obtrusive. He felt that he must seem all collar, even to the most casual eye, but he was upheld by the belief that no one would dare to mention collar to him in public. If he had sinned he was not the only sinner, for he was but a partner in conspiracy. He walked down the stairs boldly.

"And to think that his vanity should be the cause of robbing poor little Bobberts," he heard a clear voice say as he neared the dining room door. "It is too mean! I can never look up to man with the faith I have always had in man, after this. But I know they were his footprints, Laura."

"Are you so sure, Kitty?" asked Mrs. Fenelby. "Mightn't they bemightn't they be Bridget's?"

"They were not," said the voice of Kitty, and Billy paused where he was and stood still. "Bridget does not go about in the wet grass in her stocking feet. Those were Billy's tracks on the porch. I am no Sherlock Holmes, but I can tell you just what he did. He stole down before we were awake, to look for that collar, and he did not find it on the railing where he had left it. Then he saw it where it had fallen and he went down on the wet lawn and got it. Watch him when he comes in to breakfast. He will be wearing a collar, and it will not be the one he wore last night."

Billy turned and tiptoed softly up the stairs again, undoing his tie as he went. When he came down his neck was neatly, but informally swathed in a white handkerchief. Three pairs of eyes watched him as he entered, but he faced them unflinchingly. Mr. and Mrs. Fenelby let their eyes drop before his glance, but Kitty met his gaze with a challenge. There was nothing of treachery in her face, and yet she had sought to betray him. He looked at her with greater interest than he had ever known himself to feel regarding any girl, and as he looked he had a startled sense that she was fairer than she had been, and he caught his breath quickly and began to talk to Mrs. Fenelby.

"Tom," he said, after breakfast, as Mr. Fenelby was getting ready to leave to catch his train, "I think I'll walk over to the station with you. I have something I want to say to you."

"Come along," said Mr. Fenelby. "But you will have to walk quickly. I have just time to catch my train."

"Did you notice anything peculiar about Miss Kitty this morning?" asked Billy, when they had left the house.

"Peculiar?" said Mr. Fenelby. "No, I don't think so."

"Well, I don't want to make trouble, Tom," said Billy, "but I think I ought to speak about this thing. If it wasn't serious I wouldn't mention it at all, but I think you ought to know what is going on in your own house. I think you ought to know what kind of a girl Miss Kitty is, so that you can be on your guard. Now, you went down to get that collar for me, didn't you?"

"I wish you wouldn't mention that," said Mr. Fenelby with some annoyance.

"Oh, I know all about that," said Billy, warmly. "You say that because you don't like to be thanked for all these nice, thoughtful things you do for a fellow. But I do thank youjust as much as if you had found the collar and had brought it up to me. That was all right. You would have paid the duty on it, and that would have been all right. But what do you think Miss Kitty did? Why do you think you could not find that collar? Do you know what she did? She brought that collar into the housesmuggled it inand she had the nerve, the actual nerve, to give it to me. And I took it. I couldn't do anything else, could I, when a girl offered it to me? I couldn't say I wouldn't take it, could I? I had to be a gentleman about it. And then she tried to get me into trouble by telling you I would come down to breakfast wearing that collar. She tried to make out that I was a smuggler."

"I suppose it was just a bit of fun," said Mr. Fenelby. "Girls are that way, some of them."

"Well, I want it understood that that collar is in the house, and that I didn't bring it in," said Billy, "and that if this Domestic Tariff business is to be carried out fairly it is Miss Kitty's business to pay the duty on it. I want to set myself right with you. But the thing I wanted to speak about was far more serious. Do you know what she had on this morning?"

"What she had on?" asked Mr. Fenelby. "What did she have on?"

"She had on a pink shirtwaist," said Billy fiercely. "That is what she had on. Right at breakfast there, in plain sight of everyone. A pink shirtwaist!"

"Well, that's all right, isn't it?" asked Mr. Fenelby, doubtfully. "It's proper to wear a pink shirtwaist at breakfast, isn't it? I think Laura wears shirtwaists at breakfast sometimes. I'm sure it's all right. An informal home breakfast like that."

"But it was pink," insisted Billy. "I looked right at it, and I know. Real pink. You wouldn't notice it, because you are so honest yourself, and so confiding, but I noticed it the first thing. Now what do you think of your Miss Kitty? What do you say to thata girl coming right down to breakfast in a pink shirtwaist, right before the whole family?"

"II don't know what to say," faltered Mr. Fenelby, and this was the truth, for he did not.

"Well, what would you say if I told you that she had on a white shirtwaist last eveninga white one with fluffy stuff all around the collar?" asked Billy. "Wouldn't you say that that proved it?"

"I don't see anything wrong in that," said Mr. Fenelby. "What does it prove?"

"It proves that she has two shirtwaists," said Billy, seriously, "that is what it proves. Two shirtwaists, a white one and a pink one, one for dinner and one for breakfast. I don't blame you for not noticing it, but I am strong that way. I notice colors and trimmings and all that sort of thing. And I tell you she has two. I saw them both and I know it. If that isn't serious I don't know what is."

"Well?" said Mr. Fenelby.

"Well," echoed Billy, "she is only supposed to have one. She only paid duty on one, and she has two. That is what I call real smuggling. And nobody knows how many more she has. Dozens for all I know. Imagine her talking about my one poor old last year's collar, and then flaunting around in two shirtwaists right before our eyes. I call that pretty serious. I'm going to watch her. You can't be here all day to do it, but I haven't anything else to do, and I'm going to stay right around her all day and find out about this thing."

"If you don't want to" began Mr. Fenelby, remembering Billy's protestations of dislike for girls.

"I'll do my duty by you and Bobberts, old man," said Billy, generously.

"I was only going to say that Laura could look out for that sort of thing," said Mr. Fenelby. "I might say a word to her."

"Well, now, I didn't like to bring that part of it up," said Billy, "but since you mention it, I guess I had better say the whole thing. It isn't natural that a woman shouldn't notice what another woman has on, is it? They are all keen on that sort of thing. I don't say Laura is standing in with Kitty on this shirtwaist smuggling. I suppose it worries her terribly to see Kitty smuggling clothes in right under her nose, but how can Laura say anything about it? Kitty is her guest, isn't she? You leave it to me!"

Just then they reached the station and the train arrived and Mr. Fenelby jumped aboard, and as it pulled out Billy turned and walked back to the house.

VI

BRIDGET

When the Commonwealth of Bobberts had adopted the Fenelby Domestic Tariff it had been Mrs. Fenelby's duty to inform Bridget of it, and to explain it to her, and for two days Mrs. Fenelby worried about it. It was only by exercising the most superhuman wiles that a servant could be persuaded to sojourn in the suburb. To hold one in thrall it was necessary to practice the most consummate diplomacy. The suburban servant knows she is a rare and precious article, and she is apt to be headstrong and independent, and so she must be driven with a tight rein and strong hand, and yet she is so apt to leave at a moment's notice if anything offends her, that she must be driven with a light rein and a hand as light and gentle as a bit of thistledown floating on a zephyr. This is a hard combination to attain. It is like trying to drive a skittish and headstrong horse, densely constructed of lampchimneys and window glass, down a rough cobblestoned hill road. If given the rein the glass horse will dash madly to flinders, and if the rein is held taut the horse's glass head will snap off and the whole business go to crash. No juggler keeping alternate cannonballs and feathers in the air ever exercised greater nicety of calculation than did Mrs. Fenelby in her act of at once retaining and restraining Bridget.

To go boldly into the kitchen and announce to Bridget that she would hereafter be expected to pay into Bobberts' bank ten per cent. of the value of every necessity and thirty per cent. of the value of every luxury she brought into the house was the last thing that Mrs. Fenelby would have thought of doing. There were bits in that rough sketch of human nature known as Bridget's character that did not harmonize with the idea. There had been nothing said, when Bridget had been engaged, about a domestic tariff. Paying one is not usually considered a part of a general houseworker's duties, and Mrs. Fenelby felt that it would be poor policy to break this news to Bridget too abruptly. She used diplomacy.

"Bridget," she said, kindly, "we are very well satisfied with the way you do your work. We like you very well indeed."

"Thank ye, ma'am," answered Bridget, "and I'm glad to hear ye say it, though it makes little odds t' me. I do the best I know how, ma'am, and if ye don't like the way I do, there is plenty of other ladies would be glad t' get me."

"But we do like the way you do," said Mrs. Fenelby eagerly. "We are perfectly satisfiedperfectly!"

"From th' way ye started off," said Bridget, with a shrug of her shoulders, "I thought ye was goin' t' give me th' bounce. Some does it that way."

"No, indeed," Mrs. Fenelby assured her. "Especially not as you take such an interest in dear little Bobberts. You seem to like him as well as if he was your own little brother. Did I tell you what Mr. Fenelby had planned for him?"

"Somethin' t' make more worrk for me, is it?" asked Bridget suspiciously.

"Not at all!" said Mrs. Fenelby. "It is just about his education; about when he gets old enough to go to college."

"'Twill be a long time from now before then," said Bridget. "I can see it has nawthin' to do with me."

"But that is just it," said Mrs. Fenelby. "It has something to do with youand with all of us. With everyone in this house. You love little Bobberts so much that you will be glad to help in his education."

"Will I?" said Bridget in a way that was not too encouraging.

"Yes, I know you will," Mrs. Fenelby chirped cheerfully, "because it is the cutest plan. I know you will be so interested in it. Mr. Fenelby thought of it himself, and he told me to tell you about it, because, really, you know, you are just like one of the family"

"Barring I have t' be in at ten o'clock and have t' sleep in th' attic," Bridget interposed. "And don't eat with th' family. And a few other differences. But go ahead and tell me what is th' extry worrk."

"Well, it isn't extra work at all," said Mrs. Fenelby reassuringly. "It is just a way we thought of to raise money to pay for Bobberts' education. It is like a government and taxes, and everybody in the family pays part of the taxes"

"I was wonderin' why I was one of the family so much, all of a suddent," said Bridget. "I thought something was comin'. I notice that whenever I get to be one of th' family, ma'am, where ever I happen t' be workin', something comes. But it never has been taxes before. It is a new one to me, taxes is."

Mrs. Fenelby explained as clearly as she could the meaning and method of the Fenelby Domestic Tariff, and its simple schedule of rates, and Bridget listened attentively. Mrs. Fenelby expected an explosion, and was prepared for it.

"I'm sure I'm much obliged t' ye, Missus Fenelby," said Bridget, sarcastically, "an' 'tis a great honor ye are doin' me t' take me into th' family this way, but 'tis agin me principles t' be one of th' family on sixteen dollars a month when there is tariffs in th' same family. I'm thinkin' I'll stay outside th' family, ma'am. An' if ye will kindly let me past, I'll go up an' be packin' up me trunk."

"But Bridget," Mrs. Fenelby said, quickly, "I am not through yet. I knew you couldn't afford to pay thethe tariff. I didn't expect you to, out of your wages. And if you had just waited a minute I was going to tell you that, seeing that you will be out of pocket by the tariff, I am going to pay you eighteen dollars a month after this."

"Well, of course," said Bridget with a sweet smile, "I was only jokin' about me trunk."

So that was all settled, and Mrs. Fenelby felt at ease, but she did not think it necessary to tell her husband about the extra two dollars a month. It came out of her housekeeping money, and she could economize a little on something else.

"Laura," said her husband that evening, "have you spoken to Bridget about the tariff yet?"

"Yes, dear," she answered, and he said that was right, and that she must see that Bridget lived up to it. But he did not tell her that he had interviewed Bridget while Mrs. Fenelby was upstairs a few minutes before, nor that he had privately agreed with Bridget to pay her two dollars a month extra out of his own pocket provided she accepted the Fenelby Domestic Tariff, and abided by it, just as if she was one of the family. Neither did Bridget think it worth while to mention it to Mrs. Fenelby. From the time she was informed of the existence of the tariff up to the arrival of Kitty Bridget paid into Bobberts' bank twenty cents. This was the duty on a two dollar hat that even the most critical mind could not have called a luxury, and there Bridget's payments seemed to stop. She did not seem to feel the need of making any purchases just then.

"Kitty, dear," said Mrs. Fenelby, gently, the morning of the damp footprints on the porch, after the men had started for the station, "that is a pretty shirtwaist you have on this morning."

"Do you like it?" asked Kitty, innocently. "Don't you think it is a little tight across the shoulders?"

"No," said Mrs. Fenelby. "And I like this skirt better than the one you were wearing yesterday."

There was no mistaking the meaning of that. The way Mrs. Fenelby bowed over the bit of sewing she had taken up was evidence that she had suspicion in her mind. Kitty clasped her hands behind her back and laughed.

"You have been looking into my closet!" she declared. "You sit there and try to look innocent, and you know everything that I have, down to the last ribbon! Well, I just can't afford to pay your old tariff. It would simply ruin me. And the men will never know, anyway. They don't notice such things. I could wear a different dress every day, and they wouldn't know it."

"But I know it," said Laura, reprovingly. "Do you think it is right, Kitty, to smuggle things into the house that way? Is it fair to Bobberty?"

"There!" exclaimed Kitty, dropping a jingling coin into Bobberts' bank. "There is a quarter for him! That is every cent I can afford."

"That wouldn't pay the duty on one single shirtwaist," said Laura, quietly.

"It wouldn't," admitted Kitty, frankly, bending over Laura and taking her face in her hands. She turned the face upward and looked in its eyes. Then she bent down and whispered in Laura's ear, and laughed as a blush suffused Laura's face.

"I was short of money," said Laura with dignity, "and I mean to pay the duty as soon as I get my next week's allowance. I simply had to have a new purse, and you coaxed me to buy it. It wasn't smuggling at all."

"Wasn't it?" asked Kitty. "Then why did you ask me to leave it in my room, instead of showing it to Tom? Smuggler!"

Mrs. Fenelby arose and walked away. She turned to the kitchen and opened the door. She was just in time to see Bridget lower a bottle from her lips and hastily conceal it behind her skirts.

"Bridget!" she exclaimed sharply, with horror.

"'Tis th' doctor's orders, ma'am," said Bridget. "'Tis for me cold."

She coughed as well as she could, but it was not a very successful cough. Mrs. Fenelby hesitated a moment, and then she pointed to the door.

"You may pack your trunk, Bridget," she said, and Bridget jerked off her apron and stamped out of the kitchen.

"But perhaps the poor thing was taking it by her doctor's orders," suggested Kitty, when Mrs. Fenelby, red eyed, went into the front rooms again.

"She'll have to go," said Mrs. Fenelby, dolefully. "I can't have a drinking servant where poor, dear Bobberts is. But that isn't what makes me feel so badly. It is to think how that girl has deceived me. I treated her just as I would treat one of the family, and she pretended to be so fond of Bobberts, and so interested in his education, and so eager to help his fund, and here she has been smuggling liquor into the house all the time."

She wiped her eyes and sighed.

"And liquor is a luxury, and pays thirty per cent.," she said sadly. "I don't know who to trust when I can't trust a girl like Bridget. She should have paid the duty the minute she brought the stuff into the house. It just shows that you can't place any reliance on that class."

Kitty nodded assent.

"You'll have to pay her," she said. "Shall I run up and get your purse?"

She went, and as she reached the hall, Billy entered. He gazed at Kitty's garments closely, making mental note of them for future comparisons, and as he stood aside to let her pass he held one hand carefully out of sight behind him. It held a packagean oblong package, sharply rectangular in shape. A close observer would have said it was a box such as contains fifty cigars when it is full, but it was not full. Billy had taken one of the cigars out when he made the purchase at the station cigar store.

VII

THE AMATEUR DETECTIVE

When Billy Fenelby had taken his box of cigars up to his room he came down again, but he did not go anywhere near Bobberts' bank, as he should have gone had he intended depositing in it the thirty per cent. of the value of the cigars, which was the duty due on cigars under the provisions of the Fenelby Domestic Tariff. He walked out to the veranda and got into the hammock and began to read the morning paper.

From time to time he let it hang down over the edge of the hammock, as if it bored him, and he glanced at the door as if he hoped someone would come out of the house. The paper was not very interesting that morning, and Billy had other things to think of. He had volunteered to keep an eye on Kitty, and to find out definitely, if he could, whether she was smuggling shirtwaists and other things—or had already smuggled them—into the house, contrary to the provisions of the tariff. He felt that the more he saw of girls the less he liked them, and that the more he saw of Kitty, particularly, the less he fancied her, but if he was going to do this amateur detective business he wanted to begin it as soon as possible, and he watched the door closely. He wanted to see whether Kitty would still wear the pink shirtwaist she had worn at breakfast, or the white one she had worn the evening before, or whether she would dare to wear another.

The sudden departure of Bridget had upset the domestic affairs somewhat, and Kitty and Mrs. Fenelby were busy in the kitchen, but after the dishes were washed, and the rooms set to rights, and the beds made, and Bobberts given his bath, Kitty came out. It had been a long and tedious morning for Billy. There is nothing so helpless as a detective who can't work at his business of detecting, and when the job is to detect a pretty girl, and she won't show up, the waiting is rather tiresome. At one time Billy was almost tempted to go in and ask her to come out, and he would probably have gone in and snooped around a bit, if she had not appeared just then.

Kitty came out with all the brazen effrontery of a hardened criminal. That is to say she came out singing, and with her hair perfectly in order, and looking in every way fresh and charming. Billy recognized this immediately as the wile of a malefactor trying to throw an officer of the law off the scent, but he was not to be discouraged by it, and he jumped out of the hammock and went up to her. She still wore the pink shirtwaist, and it was very becoming. She looked just as well in it as if she had paid the lawful ten per cent. duty on it. It is not the duty that makes that kind of a shirtwaist pretty; it is the way it is made, and the trimming. The girl that is in it helps some, too. It is a fact that a shirtwaist looks entirely different on different girls. You have to consider the girl and her shirtwaist together, as a whole or unit, if you are going to be able to recognize it when you see it again, and Billy was ready to consider it that way. If he ever saw that pink confection with that saucy chin and merry face above it again he meant to be able to recognize the combination. That is one of the duties of a detective.

"Let's go out under the tree," he said, "and sit down, andand talk it over. I have something I want to talk about."

"Talk it over," said Kitty, lifting her eyebrows. "Talk what over?"

You couldn't nonplus Billy that way, when he was in pursuit of his duty.

"Well," he said, "wethat is, I didn't thank you for bringing me up that collar this morning. I want to thank you for it."

"Yes?" said Kitty. "Well, here I am. Thank me. You did thank me once, but I don't care. Do it again."

"Thank you," said Billy.

"You're welcome," Kitty said, and then they both laughed.

"What do you think of this Domestic Tariff business?" asked Billy, seeking to lead her into some admission of which he could make use as proof of her smuggling.

"I think it is a simply splendid idea!" Kitty declared. "I am sure no one but Tom could have thought of it, and the very minute I heard of it I went into it body and soul. It was so clever of him to conceive such an idea, and such a simple way to build up an education fund for dear, sweet, little Bobberts! And isn't it nice of Tom and Laura to let us be in it and pay our share of the duty. It makes us feel so much more as if we were really part of the family."

"Doesn't it?" said Billy. "It makes us feel as if we had a right to be herewhen we pay duty and all that. I feel like bringing in a lot of stuff just so that I can pay duty on it. I was thinking about it this morning, and about that little joke of mine about not bringing in that collar last night, and I felt what I had missed by leaving it out on the porch, so I got up and went down for it. That was how you happened to meet me in the hallI wanted to get it and bring it in so I could pay the duty, and be in the fun myself. You don't think I was going to smuggle it in, do you?"

"Oh, no!" said Kitty, with a longdrawn o. "Nobody would be so mean as to smuggle anything into the house, when the duty all goes to dear little Bobberts. It is such fun to pay duty, just as if the house was a real nation. It is like being part of the nation, and you know we women are not that. We can't vote, nor anything, and a chance like this is so rare that we enjoy it immensely. You didn't think it was queer that I should go down so early in the morning to get your collar and bring it in, did you?"

"Well, of course," said Billy, doubtfully, "it wasn't your collar, you know. It was my collar."

"I know it was," Kitty admitted frankly, "but you know how little we women can bring into the house. Hardly anything. We shop and shop, but we hardly ever really buy anything, and all the time I am just crazy to be paying duty, and to know whether it is ten per cent. or thirty per cent., and all that, as if I was a man, and so, when I happened to think of that collar that you had left down here on the porch railing, I saw it was my chance, and I decided to come down and get it and bring it into the house, so I could have the fun of paying the duty on it. So I came down and got it. And just as I reached the landing on my way up I met you, and I was so surprised that I just handed the collar to you."

"Of course," said Billy. "That was just the way it was, except that I had just reached the landing on my way up, when you handed me the collar. You couldn't have just reached the landing, because if you had we would have been going up the stairs together, side by side, and we were not doing that. I was going up the stairs, and just as I reached the landing you came from somewhere and handed me the collar."

"Isn't that what I said?" asked Kitty sweetly. "It amounts to the same thing, anyway, doesn't it? I had the collar, and you got it. I suppose you paid the duty on it?"

"Me?" said Billy. "Not much! I didn't bring it into the house; you brought it in. You have to pay the duty."

"I pay the duty on your collar?" laughed Kitty. "Well, I should think I would not! I went down and got it for you, and that was nothing but an act of kindness that anybody would do for anybody else. You can pay your own duties."

"Oh, I sha'n't pay a duty on it!" scoffed Billy. "I didn't want the collar. I didn't need it, and I refused to bring it into the house on principle. I don't believe in tariff duties. I'm a free trader. I wouldn't smuggle, and I wouldn't pay duty, and so I left it outside. You should have left it there. You didn't leave it there, and so it is your duty to pay the duty."

"Never!" declared Kitty.

For a few minutes they were silent, and Billy looked glumly at the street. Then he cheered up suddenly. He looked at Kitty and smiled.

"I'll tell you what let's do!" he exclaimed. "Let's go out under the tree and talk it over. We'll go out under the tree and talk it all over. That is the only way we can settle it."

"It is settled now," said Kitty. "I don't think it needs any more settling."

Billy beamed upon her cheerfully.

"Well," he said, "let's go out under the tree andand unsettle it."

For a moment Kitty seemed to hesitate, but that was only for Billy's good, lest he think she yielded to his whims too readily. Then she went, and draped herself gracefully upon the sweet, dry grass, and Billy sat himself crosslegged near her.

"Now, what do you think of this Domestic Tariff business, anyway?" he asked.

"I think it is the silliest thing I ever heard of," said Kitty frankly. "I never heard of a man with real sense conceiving such a thing. As if such a lot of nonsense is needed to save a few dollars for an education that isn't to come about for sixteen years or so! And the idea of making his guests pay the duty too! It is the most unhospitable thing I ever heard of!"

"Isn't it?" agreed Billy, promptly. "It makes us feel as if we had no right to be here. A man can't afford to bring even the things he needs, when he has to pay that exorbitant duty on everything. And it is so much worse on you. Now I can get along with very little. A man can, you know. But how is a girl going to do without all the things she is accustomed to? I believe," he said, confidentially lowering his voice and glancing at the house, "I believe, if I were a girl, I would be tempted to smuggle in the things I really needed."

"Would you?" asked Kitty, sweetly. "But then you men have different ideas of such things, don't you? You don't think a girl would do such a thing, do you? Would you advise it? I don't know whetherhow would you go about smuggling, if you wanted to? But I don't believe it would be honest, would it?"

She turned up to him two such innocent eyes that Billy almost blushed. There is no satisfaction in knowing a person is guilty, the satisfaction is in making the person look guilty, and Kitty looked like an innocent child questioning the face of a tempter and seeing guilt there. He longed to ask her outright how she happened to have a pink shirtwaist, but he did not dare to, lest he put her at once on her guard. He felt a great desire to take her by the shoulders and shake her out of her calm superiority. It was very trying to him. No girl had a right to act as if she thought herself the superior of any man. Just to show her how inferior she was he dropped the subject of the tariff entirely and began a conversation on Ibsen. He did not know much about Ibsen but he knew a little and he could lead her beyond her depths and make her feel her inferiority that way. Kitty listened to him with an amused smile, and then told him a few things about Ibsen, quoted a few enlightening pages from Hauptmann, routed him, slaughtered him gently as he fled from position to position, and ended by asking him if he had ever read anything of Ibsen's. It was very trying to Billy. This girl evidently had no respect for the superior brain of man whatever.

"I think the lawn needs sprinkling," he said, coldly.

"Do you know how it should be done?" she asked, and that was the final insult. Nice girls never asked such questions in such a way. Nice girls looked up with wonder in their eyes and said, "Oh! You men know how to do everything!" That settled Billy's opinion of Kitty! She was evidently one of these overeducated, forward, scheming, coquetting girls. She had not even said, "Oh! don't sprinkle the lawn now; stay here and talk with me." He squared his shoulders and marched over to the sprinkling apparatus, while she sat with her back against the tree and watched him. He turned on the water and adjusted the nozzle to a good strong flow. He wet the lawn at the rear of the house first, and was pulling the hose after him into the front lawn when Mrs. Fenelby suddenly appeared on the porch. She had a box of cigars in her hand, and when he saw them Billy jumped guiltily.

"Billy!" she exclaimed, "Are these your cigars?"

"Why, say!" he said, after one glance at her face on which suspicion was but too plainly imprinted. "Those are cigars, aren't they? That's a whole box of cigars, isn't it?"

"It is," said Mrs. Fenelby, severely, "and I found it in your room. I don't remember having received any duty on a box of cigars, Billy. I hope you were not trying to smuggle them in. I hope you were not trying to rob poor, dear little Bobberts, Billy."

Billy held the nozzle limply in one hand and let the stream pour wastefully at his feet.

"That box of cigars" he began weakly. "That box of cigars, the box you found in my room, well, that is a box of cigars. You see, Mrs. Fenelby," he continued, cautiously, "that box of cigars was up there in my room, andNow, you know I wouldn't try to smuggle anything in, don't you? Now, I'll tell you all about it." But he didn't. He looked at the box thoughtfully. He saw now that he had been silly to buy a whole box. A man should not buy more than a handful at a time.

"Well?" said Mrs. Fenelby, impatiently.

"Isn't that the box you bought when you went over to the station with Tom this morning?" asked Kitty, sweetly. "You brought back a box when you returned you know."

Billy turned his head and glared at her. But she only smiled at him. He did not dare to look Mrs. Fenelby in the eye.

"Tom smokes a great deal, doesn't he?" Kitty continued lightly. "I wondered when you brought that box of cigars back with you if he hadn't asked you to bring them over for him. That was what I thought the moment I saw you with them."

"Why, yes, of course," said Billy, with relief. "That was how it was. II didn't like to say it, you know," he assured Mrs. Fenelby, eagerly, "II didn't know just how Tom would feel about it. Tom will pay the duty. When he comes home this evening. He couldn't come home from the stationand miss his trainand all that sort of thingjust to pay the duty on a box of cigars, could he? So I brought them home. It is perfectly plain and simple! You see if he doesn't pay the duty as soon as he gets in the house. Tom wouldn't want to smuggle them in, Mrs. Fenelby. You shouldn't think he would do such a thing. I'mI'm surprised that you should think that of Tom."

Mrs. Fenelby looked at him doubtfully, and then glanced at Kitty's innocent face. She shook her head. It did not seem just what Tom would have done, but she could not deny that it might be so. She would know all about it when he came home in the evening. She cast a glance at the lawn, and uttered a cry. Billy was pouring oceans of water at full pressure upon her pansy bed, and the poor flowers were dashing madly about and straining at their roots. Some were already lying washed out by the roots. Billy looked, and swung the nozzle sharply around, and the scream that Kitty uttered told him that he had hit another mark. That pink shirtwaist looked disreputable. Water was dripping from all its laces, and from Kitty's hair, and her cheeks glistened with pearly drops. She was drenched.

"Goodness!" she exclaimed, shaking her hanging arms and her downbent head, and then glancing at Billy, who stood idiotically regarding her, she laughed. He was a statue of miserable regret, and the limply held garden hose was pouring its stream unheeded into his low shoes. Wet as she was, and uncomfortable, she could not refrain from laughing, for Billy could not have looked more guilty if she had been sugar and had completely melted before his eyes. Even Mrs. Fenelby laughed.

"It doesn't matter a bit!" said Kitty, reassuringly. "Really, I don't mind it at all. It was nice and cool."

She was very pretty, from Billy's point of view, as she stood with a wisp or two of wet hair coquettishly straggling over her face. Mrs. Fenelby would have said she looked mussy, but there is something strangely enticing to a man in a bit of hair wandering astray over a pretty face. Before marriage, that is. It quite finished Billy. He forgave her all just on account of those few wet, wandering locks.

"I'm so sorry!" he said, with enormous contrition. "I'm awfully sorry. I'mI'm mighty sorry. Really, I'm sorry."

"Now, it doesn't matter a bit," said Kitty lightly. "Not a bit! I'll just run up and get on something dry"

"You had better shut off the water," said Mrs. Fenelby, and went into the house.

Billy laid the hose carefully at his feet.

"I say," he said, hesitatingly, to Kitty, "wear the one you had on last nightthe white one. II think that one's pretty."

"Oh, no!" said Kitty. "I can't wear that one. That one is all mussed up. I can't wear that one again. I have a lovely blue one."

"No!" said Billy, whispering, and glancing suspiciously at the house. "Not blue! Please don't! Itit's dangerous."

"Oh, but it is a dream of a waist!" said Kitty. "You wait until you see it."

"No!" pleaded Billy again. "Not a blue one! If you wore a blue one I couldn't help but notice it was blue. It isn't safe. Don't wear a blue one, or a green one, or a brown one. Just a white one. Not any other color; just white. You see," he said with sudden confidentiality, "I'm a detective. I'm detecting for Tom. I told him I would, and I've got to keep my word. He has a notion someone is smuggling things into the house without paying the duty, and he got me to detect at you for him. We're suspicious about your clothes. There's a white waist, and this pink waist, already, and if you go to wearing blue ones and all sorts of colors, I can't help but notice it. I don't want to get you into trouble with Tom, you know." He hesitated a moment and then said, "You helped me out about those cigars."

"All right!" said Kitty, cheerfully, "I'll wear a white one, but I think you might be color blind if you really want to help me."

VIII

THE FIELD OF DISHONOR

There was a train from the city at 6:02, and Tom was not likely to be home on one earlier. At 5:48 Kitty and Billy and Mrs. Fenelby were sitting on the porch, and Bobberts was lying in a tiltedback rocking chair, behaving himself. It was a calm and peaceful suburban scenethe stillness and the loneliness and the mosquitoes were all present. It was the idle time when no one cares whether time flies or halts. Mrs. Fenelby had the table set and the cold dinner ready; Kitty was primped; and Billy should have had nothing in the world to do, but he had been opening and closing his watch every minute for the last half hour. He was uneasy. At 5:48 he arose and stretched out his arms.

"I guess," he said as lazily as he could; "I guess I'll walk down and meet Tom. I haven't been out much today."

There was one thing he had to do. He had to see Tom before Mrs. Fenelby could see him, and explain about that box of cigars. If Tom was to be held responsible for the duty on it Tom should at least know that a box of cigars had been brought into the house. It was absolutely necessary for Billy to see Tom, and explain a few things.

"We have none of us been out enough today," said Mrs. Fenelby. "It will do us all good to walk down to the station, and we will take Bobberts."

Billy stood still. The cheerful expression that had rested on his face faded. There would be a pretty lot of trouble if the whole lot of them went in a group, and he wondered that Kitty did not see this, and why she did not say something to dissuade Mrs. Fenelby from leaving the house. He simply had to get a few words with Tom in private before Mrs. Fenelby could ask her husband about the cigars.

"When the 6:02 pulled in" "When the 6:02 pulled in"
"I wouldn't advise it," said Billy, shaking his head. "No, indeed. I wouldn't take the chance, Laura." He walked to the end of the porch and peered earnestly at the western sky. It was a singularly clear and cloudless sky. "I'm afraid it will rain," he explained, boldly. "It wouldn't do to take Bobberts out and let him get rained on. It looks just like one of those evenings when a rain comes up all of a sudden. I wouldn't risk it."

"Nonsense!" said Mrs. Fenelby, shortly, and she gathered the crowing Bobberts into her arms and started. Kitty also arose, but Billy hung back.

"I guess I won't go," he declared. "It looks too much like rain."

"Nonsense!" declared Mrs. Fenelby again. "You come right along. I don't believe it will rain for a week."

There was nothing for him to do but to go, and he went. The three of them were standing on the platform when the 6:02 pulled in, and they looked eagerly for Mr. Fenelby, but they did not see him among the alighting commuters. Mr. Fenelby saw them first. He saw them before the train pulled up to the station, for he had been standing on the car platform with a box under his arm, ready to make a dash for home the moment the train stopped, but now he stepped back and, as the train slowed down, he jumped off on the opposite side of the train. There was a small row of evergreens on the little lawn of the station, and he stepped behind one of them and waited. Between the thin branches of the tree he could see his family, when the train pulled out, looking eagerly at the straggling line of commuters. The box he held was heavy, and he hoped the family would soon decide that he had missed the train, and would go home, but he saw Mrs. Fenelby seat herself on the waitingbench. He saw Kitty take a seat beside her, and he saw Billy, after evident hesitation, take the seat next to Kitty. The evergreen tree was small, and the next tree to it was ten feet distant. He was marooned behind that tree.

Mr. Fenelby instantly saw that he had done a foolish thing. He had that overwhelming sense of foolishness that comes to a man at times, when he thinks he has never done a sane and sound act in his whole silly life. Mr. Fenelby realized that he had been foolish when he had bought, on the subscription plan, a complete set of Eugene Field's works, bound in threequarters levant morocco, twelve volumes for thirtysix dollars. He realized that although he had had to pay but five dollars down, to the agent, he would have to pay thirty per cent. of the value of the whole set, in duty, the moment he took the books into the house. He realized that he had been silly to bring the whole heavy set home at one time. He realized that he had been positively childish when he thought of hiding himself behind this miserable little tree, with this heavy box in his arms and six suburban stores staring him full in the face. He wondered what the proprietors of the six stores would think of him if they happened to see him hiding there behind the tree, while his whole family awaited him on the station platform. And then, as he happened to remember that one of the stores was a drugstore with a sodafountain, he shuddered. Given three suburbanites on a station platform, and a train not due for thirty minutes for which they must wait, and a sodafountain across the way, and the answer is that the three suburbanites will soon be in the place where the sodafountain is.

When Mrs. Fenelby arose Mr. Fenelby shifted the box of books into a more secure angle of his arm, and as the trio, and Bobberts, started across the track and lawn Mr. Fenelby edged cautiously around the tree to keep it between him and them. The trade of smuggler has ever been one of wild adventure and excitement.

He peered at them until they entered the drugstore, and then he backed cautiously away, step by step, with the tree as a screen. As he reached the corner of the station he turned and ran, and as he turned he saw Billy hurry out of the drugstore and run, and Mrs. Fenelby and Kitty hurry out after Billy. Mr. Fenelby did not wait to see if they also ran. He ran all the way home, and hurried into the house, and up the stairs to the attic. He felt better about the set of Field now. He had always wanted it, and he deserved it, for he had waited for it long. He could hide it in the attic and bring it into the realm of the tariff duty one volume at a time. He felt his way into the fartherest corner and pushed the box under the rafters. It would not quite go back where he wanted it to go, for something was in the way of it. He pulled the other thing out. It was also a box. It was another box of Eugene Field in twelve volumes, threequarter levant, and it was addressed to "Mrs. Thomas Fenelby." There had never been any duty paid on books since the Commonwealth of Bobberts had been established. For a moment Mr. Fenelby frowned angrily; then he smiled. He hid his set of Field in the other corner of the attic, and hurried down stairs.

He expected to find Billy there, for he had seen him start to run when he left the drugstore, but there was no Billy in sight, and Mr. Fenelby seated himself in the hammock and waited. He was ready to receive his returning family with an easy conscience. His box was well hidden. When they appeared in the distance he saw that they were all together, Billy and the two girls and Bobberts, and Mr. Fenelby arose and waved his hand to them. He was ready to be merry and jovial, and to tease them cheerfully because they had not seen him when he got off the train. But Mrs. Fenelby climbed the porch steps with an air of anger.

"Good evening," she said, coldly. "I see you are home."

She laid Bobberts in the chair and faced Mr. Fenelby.

"Now, I want to know what all this means!" she declared. "I think there is something peculiar going on in this family. Why did Billy run all the way down to the next station so that he could be the first to meet you as you came home this evening? Why did you avoid us at the station and hurry home this way? You may think I am simple, Thomas Fenelby, but I believe somebody is smuggling things into the house without paying the tariff duty on them! I believe you and Billy are conspiring to rob poor, dear little Bobberts, and I want to know the truth about it! I believe Kitty is in it too!"

"Laura!" exclaimed Kitty, with horror, recoiling from her, while the two men stood sheepishly. "Why, Laura Fenelby! If you say such a thing I shall go right up and pack my clothes and go home!"

"What clothes?" asked Mr. Fenelby, meaningly. Kitty ignored the insinuation.

"You three should not dare to look me in the face and talk about smuggling," she declared. "You dare to accuse me. I would like to have you explain about that box upstairs first."

Mr. Fenelby and Billy and Mrs. Fenelby paled. For one moment there was perfect silence while Kitty, with folded arms, looked at them scornfully. Then, with strange simultaneousness, all three opened their mouths and said:

"I'll explain about that box!"

IX

BOBBERTS INTERVENES

Kitty stood scornfully triumphant awaiting the next words of the guilty trio, and three more cowed and guiltstricken smugglers never faced an equally guilty accuser with such uncomfortable feelings. Billy was sorry he had ever tried to fabricate the story about Mr. Fenelby having asked him to bring the box of cigars home; Mr. Fenelby wished he had left the set of Eugene Field's works at the office, and Mrs. Fenelby was, perhaps, the most worried of all, for she did not know whether to admit her guilt and own that she had brought a set of Eugene Field into the house without paying the duty, or to annihilate the accusing Kitty by declaring that Kitty had a whole closet full of smuggled garments. It was a trying situation.

In a drama this would have been the cue for the curtain to fall with a rush, ending the act and leaving the audience a space to wonder how the complication could ever be untangled, but on the Fenelby's porch there was no curtain to fall. So Bobberts fell instead.

He raised his pink hands and his head, rolled over in the porch rocker in which he had been lying, and fell to the porch floor with a bump. A curtain could not have ended the scene more quickly. Never in his life had he been so cruelly treated as by this faithless rockingchair. He had reposed his simple faith in it, and it threw him to earth, and then rocked joyously across him. His voice arose in short, piercing yells. He turned purple with rage and pain. He drew up his knees and simply, soulfully screamed. Up and down the street neighbors came out upon their verandas, napkins in hand, and stared wonderingly at the Fenelby porch. Kitty and Billy stood like a wooden Mr. and Mrs. Noah in the toy ark, but Mr. Fenelby and Laura sprang to Bobberts' aid and gathered him into their arms, ordering each other to do things, and soothing Bobberts at the same time.

The Fenelby Domestic Tariff was entirely forgotten.

"Well!" exclaimed Mrs. Fenelby, when Bobberts had tapered off from the yells of rage to the steady weeping of injured feelings. "What are you standing there like two sticks for? Can't you see poor, dear little Bobberts is nearly killed? Why don't you do something?"

There was really nothing they could do. Mr. and Mrs. Fenelby made such a compact crowd around Bobberts that no one else could squeeze in, but Kitty dropped on her knees and edged up to the crowd, murmuring, "Poor Bobberts! Poor Bobberts!"

Billy stood awkwardly, feeling in his pockets. He had an idea that if he could find something to jingle before Bobberts it might be about the right thing to do, but his hand touched one of the smuggled cigars, and he withdrew it as if his fingers had been burnt. This poor, weeping child was the Bobberts he had been cheating of a few pennies. He touched Kitty diffidently on the shoulder.

"Can't I do something?" he asked, pleadingly, and Kitty took pity on him.

"Heat some water; very hot!" she said. She was not a baby expert, but she felt that hot water would not be a bad thing to have handy in a case like this. There is one good thing about hot water—if it is not wanted it does no harm, for if allowed to stand it will get cool again—and it pleased her to be able to order Billy to do something. The prompt and eager manner in which he obeyed the order pleased her still more. He ran all the way to the kitchen.

Half an hour later he cautiously carried a dishpan full of water to the porch and stared in amazement at the place where he had left Bobberts and his parents. They were gone! He felt that he had not been quite as quick with the water as he might have been, for the only burner that had been lighted on the gas range was the "simmerer," and that had only a flame as large around as a dollar, and not strong, but he had not dared to light another. He had a dim remembrance that stoves of some kind sometimes exploded, and he did not want to risk an explosion by tampering with an unknown stove. He felt that a stove and Bobberts both exploding at the same time would have been more than the Fenelbys could have borne. As he stood holding the pan of hot water well away from him the sound of the click of knives and forks on china came to him through the open window. Only a little of the hot water spilled over the edge of the pan upon his legs as he opened the screen door and entered the hall.

He walked carefully, bent over and holding the pan at arm's length, and as he entered the dining room the three diners looked up at him in open mouthed surprise. They had forgotten all about Billy.

"Here it is," said Billy, with modest pride and an air of accomplishment. "It is good and hot. I let it get as hot as it could."

The blank amazement that had dulled the face of Kitty gave way to a look of understanding and a smile as she remembered having ordered him to get hot water, but the amazement on the faces of Mr. Fenelby and his wife remained as blank as ever.

"It is hot water," said Billy, explaining. "I heated it. What shall I do with it?"

The sodden surprise on Mr. Fenelby's face melted away. A dishpan full of hot water served during the course of a cold dinner had amusing elements, and Mr. Fenelby smiled. So did Mrs. Fenelby. Everybody smiled but Billy. He was serious.

"Well," he said, with a touch of impatience, "these handles are hot. I can't stand here holding them all night. What do you want me to do with this hot water?"

"What do you want to do with it?" asked Mr. Fenelby. "What do you usually do with a panful of hot water when you have one? You might take a bath, if you want to. You will find the bathroom at the top of the stairs, first turn to the left. Run along, and don't stay in the water too long."

Mrs. Fenelby and Kitty laughed, and Mr. Fenelby smiled broadly at his own humor. Billy blushed.

"I heated it for Bobberts," he said, stiffly.

"Thank you!" said Mr. Fenelby. "But we won't boil Bobberts this evening, Billy. Not just now, anyhow. We like to oblige, but we can't be expected to boil our only son just because you turn up in the middle of a meal with a pan of hot water. If we ever boil him it will not be in the middle of a meal. Please don't insist."

Billy reddened to the roots of his hair. Mrs. Fenelby was laughing openly and Tom was pleased with the excellence of his joke. Billy raised his head angrily and strode out of the room, and Kitty, from whose face the smile had fled, started up with blazing eyes.

"I think you are horrid!" she cried, turning to Bobberts' laughing parents. "I think you ought to thank him instead of making fun of him. I told him to heat the water, because Bobberts was hurt, and I thought you might want it, and because he was trying to be helpful andand nice, you sit there and laugh at him. If you want to make fun of anyone, make fun of me! I suppose you will!"

"Why, Kitty!" cried Mrs. Fenelby.

"Yes!" cried Kitty. "I suppose you will. That seems to be what you want to domake your guests as uncomfortable as you can. You don't want us here. You make up this foolish tariff to make trouble, and you drive away your servants so that we feel that we are imposing on you, and you make fun of us when we try to be helpful"

"Why, Kitty!" exclaimed Mrs. Fenelby again.

"You do!" Kitty declared. "I'm surprised at you, Laura Fenelby, I am indeed. I'm surprised that you should let your husband dictate to you, and make you his slave with his tariffs and such things, but you like it. Very well, be his slave if you want to. But I can see one thingBilly and I are not wanted in this house. You and your husband just want to be alone and enjoy your selfish house. The best thing Billy and I can do is to go. I can see very plainly now, Laura, that you got up that silly tariff just to drive us out of the house. Very well, we will go!"

She turned from the amazed parents of Bobberts to the amazed Billy who was standing in the hall with the inoffensive pan of hot water in his hands, and put her hand on his arm.

"Come!" she said. "I am going up to pack my trunks."

For a moment after the shock the Fenelbys sat in surprised silence, looking blankly each into the other's face, and then Laura spoke.

"Tom," she gasped, "they mustn't leave this way!"

Mr. Fenelby slowly folded his napkin, and as slowly placed it in the ring. Then he laid the ring gently on the table and arranged his knife and fork side by side on his plate, as prescribed by the guide books to good manners.

"She said she was going up stairs to pack her trunks," he said with deliberation. "To pack her trunks. If she has enough to pack into trunks, Laura, there has been smuggling going on in this house."

Mrs. Fenelby folded her napkin as slowly as her husband had just folded his, and she kept her eyes on it as she answered.

"Tom," she said, "do you think it is quite the time now to talk of smuggling? Wouldn't it be better if you went up and apologized to Kitty and Billy?"

"Laura," said Mr. Fenelby, "it is always time to talk of smuggling. The foundation of the home is order; order can only be maintained by living up to such rules as are made; the Fenelby Domestic Tariff is more than a rule, it is a law. If we let the laws of our home be trampled under foot by whoever chooses the whole thing totters, sways and falls. The home is wrecked and sorrow and dissention come. Dissention leads to misunderstanding and divorce. That is why I am strict. That is why I refuse to let two strangers wreck our whole lives by ignoring the Domestic Tariff. If they do not like the laws of our little Commonwealth, they can go. The door is open!"

"Thomas Fenelby," said his wife, "I think you are horrid! I never knew anything so unhospitable in my life. It isn't as if no one in this house ever broke that tariff law except Kitty and Billy; you haven't explained about that box"

Mr. Fenelby reddened and he looked at his wife sternly.

"Do you mean the box I found hidden under the eaves in the attic, addressed to you, my dear?" he asked with cutting sweetness, and Mrs. Fenelby, in turn, grew red and gasped.

"You are mean!" she exclaimed. "I think you are notnot nice to go poking around under eaves and things, trying to find some blame to throw up to your wife! I wish you had never thought of your horrid tariff, andand"

She put her handkerchief to her eyes, and a minute later went out of the room and up the stairs. Mr. Fenelby heard her cross the floor above him, and heard the creaking of the bed as she threw herself upon it. He looked sternly out of the dining room window awhile. Never, never had his wife spoken such words to him before. If she wished to act so it was very wellshe should be taught a lesson. She was vexed because she had been caught in a palpable case of smuggling herself. Now he

He arose and took Bobberts' bank from the mantel; from his pocket he drew a small collection of loose change and one or two small bills, and saving out one dime he fed the rest into Bobberts' bank. For a few more minutes he looked gloomily from the window, and then he went gloomily forth and dropped into the hammock.

With cautious steps Billy Fenelby stole down the stairs and bending over the rail looked into the dining room. It was empty, and he tiptoed down the rest of the way and, glancing from side to side like one fearing discovery, dropped a handful of loose coins into Bobberts' bank. As he ascended the stairs his face wore the look of a man who is square with the world.

As she heard the door close upon him when he entered his room Mrs. Fenelby rose from her bed and wiped her eyes. She took her purse from the dresser and opened it, then paused for she heard a door opening slowly. She heard light steps cross the hall and descend the stairs, but she could not see Kitty. She could only hear the faint click of coin dropping upon coin in the dining room below her. She knew that Kitty was feeding Bobberts' education fund, and she waited until she heard Kitty's door close again, and then she went down and poured into the opening of the bank the remains of her week's household allowance, and began the task of clearing the table. As she worked the tears splattered down upon the plates as she bent over them. How could Tom be so cruel and unfeeling? Doubtless he was enjoying the thought of having hurt her feelings, if he had not already forgotten all about her, taking his ease in the hammock.

She glanced out of the window at him. There he lay, but as she looked he raised his hands and struck himself twice on the head with his clenched fists and groaned like a man in misery. For a moment he lay still and then once more he struck himself on the head, and drawing up his legs kicked them out angrily, like a naughty child in a tantrum. He was not having the most blissful moments of his life. Once more he drew up his legs and kicked, and the hammock turned over and dumped him on the floor of the porch.

“Ouch!” he exclaimed quite normally, and looking up he saw his wife, and smiled. She not only smiled, but laughed, somewhat hysterically but forgivingly.

X

TARIFF REFORM

If a man really likes to wipe dishes, while his wife washes them, there is no better time for friendly confidences, and for the arrangement of difficulties. Diplomatists win their greatest battles for peace at the dinnertable, because the dinnertable gives abundant opportunity for the "interruption politic." When the argument reaches the fatal climax, and the final ultimatum is delivered, a boiled potato may still avert war: "Now, me lud, I ask you finally, will your government, or won't it? That is the question," and from the opposing diplomat come the words, "Beg pardon, your ludship, but will you kindly pass me the salt? Thanks! Don't you think the butter is a little strong?" and war is averted. Postponed, at least.

Just so over the dishwiping; the hard and fast logic of who's right and who's wrong is interrupted and turned aside by timely ejaculations of: "Oh, I did wipe that cup!" or interpolated questions, as: "Have you washed this plate yet, my dear?" A wise man who finds himself cornered can always drop one of the blownglass tumblers on the floorthey only cost five centsor ask, innocently: "Did I crack this plate, or was it already cracked?" By a judicious use of these little wreckers of consecutive speech Mr. and Mrs. Fenelby, over the dishes, reached a perfect understanding and forgot their quarrel. Mr. Fenelby said she was perfectly right in hiding the set of Eugene Field in the attic, since it was intended as a surprise for him on the anniversary of their wedding, and the payment of the tariff duty on it would have divulged the secret; and Mrs. Fenelby agreed that he was doing exactly the right thing when he did the same, and for the same reason; but they both agreed that Kitty and Billy had acted rather shamelessly in the matter of smuggling.

"I know Billy," said Mr. Fenelby, "and I know him well. I won't say anything about Kitty, for she is your guest, but Billy would smuggle anything he could lay his hands on. He is a lawyer, and a young one, and all you have to do is to show a young lawyer a law, and he immediately begins to look for ways to get around it. I don't say this to excuse him. I just say it."

"Well, you know how women are," said Mrs. Fenelby. "As sure as you get two or three women who have been abroad into a group they will begin telling how and what they were able to smuggle in when they came through the custom house. Some of them enjoy the smuggling part better than all the rest of their trips abroad, so what could you expect of Kitty when she had a perpetual custom house to smuggle things through? She looks on it as a sort of game, and the one that smuggles the most is the winner. I don't say this to excuse her. But it is so."

"I am not the least sorry that Billy is offended, if he is," said Mr. Fenelby, between plates; "but if you wish I will apologize to Kitty, although I don't see why I should. The thing I am worrying about is Bobberts. I like this tariff plan, and I think it is a good way to raise moneyif anyone ever pays the tariff dutiesbut I don't feel as if I was treating Bobberts right. Every time I put money in his bank in payment of the tariff duty on a thing I have brought into the house I feel that I am doing Bobberts a wrong. And the more I put in the more guilty I feel."

"Of course it is all for his education fund," said Mrs. Fenelby.

"I know it," said Mr. Fenelby, "and that is what makes me feel so small and miserable when I pay my ten or thirty per cent. duty. Bobberts is my only son, and the dearest and sweetest baby that ever lived, and I ought to be glad to give money for his education fund voluntarily and freely; and yet we treat him as if we hated him and had to be forced to give him a few cents a day. We act as if he was nothing but a government treasury deficit, and instead of giving joyously and gladly because we love him, we act as if we had to have laws made to force us to give. I feel it more every time I have to pay tariff duty into his bank. I tell you, Laura, it isn't treating Bobberts in the right spirit. If he could understand he would be hurt and offended to think his parents were the kind that had to be compelled to give him an education, as if he were a reformatory child or a Home for something or other. Any tax is always unpopular, and that means it is annoying and vexatious; and what I am afraid of is that we will get to dislike Bobberts because we feel we are injuring him. I don't mind the tariff, myself, but I do want to be fair and square with Bobberts. He's the only child we have, Laura."

"Oh, Tom!" exclaimed Mrs. Fenelby, taking her hands out of the dish water; "do you think we have gone too far to make it all right again? Do you think we have hurt our love for him, or weakened it, oror anything? If I thought so I should never, never forgive myself!"

"I hope we haven't," said Mr. Fenelby, seriously; "but we must not take any more chances. If this thing goes on we will become quite hardened toward Bobberts, and cease to love him altogether."

"We will stop this tariff right this very minute!" cried Mrs. Fenelby joyously. "I am so glad, Tom. I just hated the old thing!"

Mr. Fenelby shook his head slowly and Mrs. Fenelby's face lost its radiance and became questioningly fearstruck.

"What is it?" she asked, anxiously. "Can't we stop? Must we keep on with it forever and forever?"

"You forget the Congress of the Commonwealth of Bobberts," said Mr. Fenelby. "The tariff law was passed by the congress, and it can only be repealed by the congress, with Bobberts present."

Mrs. Fenelby wiped her hands hurriedly and rapidly untied her apron.

"I hate to waken Bobberts," she said, "but I will! I'd do anything to have that tariff unpassed again."

Mr. Fenelby put his hand on her arm, restraining her as she was about to rush from the kitchen.

"Wait, Laura!" he said. "You forget that you and I are not the only States now. Kitty and Billy are States, too. You and I would not form a quorum. We must have Kitty and Billy."

"Tom," she said, "I will get Kitty and Billy if I have to drag them in by main force!" and she went to find them. Ten minutes later she returned but without them. Mr. Fenelby had finished the dishes, and was hanging the dishpan on its nail.

The two needed States were nowhere to be found, neither in the house, nor on the porch, nor were they on the grounds. There was nothing to do but to await their return. It was quite late when Kitty and Billy returned, and the Fenelbys had grown tired of sitting on the porch and had gone inside, but Kitty and Billy did not seem to mind the dampness or the chill for the moon was beautiful, and they seated themselves in the hammock. Bobberts had been put to bed, and his parents had become almost merry with their oldtime merriment as they contemplated the speedy overthrow of the Fenelby Domestic Tariff. The joy that comes from a tax repealed is greater than the peace that comes from paying a tax honestly. There is no fun in paying taxes. Not the least.

"I think, Laura," said Mr. Fenelby, when he and his wife had listened to the slow creaking of the hammock hooks for some minutes, "you had better go out and tell them to come in."

Mrs. Fenelby went. She let the porch screen slam as she went out—which was only fair—and she heard the low whispers change to louder tones, and a slight movement of feet; but she was not, evidently, intruding, for Kitty and Billy were quite primly disposed in the hammock when she reached them.

"Hello!" she said pleasantly, "Won't you come in? We are going to vote on the tariff."

"Go ahead and vote," said Billy cheerfully. "We won't interfere."

"But we can't vote until you come in," explained Mrs. Fenelby. "We haven't a quorum until you come in. You are States, and we can't do anything until you come in."

"Did you try?" asked Billy, just as cheerfully as before. "We don't want to vote. We are comfortable out here. If we must vote, bring your congress out here."

"Billy, I would if I could," said Mrs. Fenelby,"but I can't! Bobberts has to be present, and he can't be brought out into the night air."

Kitty half rose from the hammock. She felt to see that her hair was in order.

"Come on, Billy," she said. "Be accommodating," and they went in.

It was necessary to bring Bobberts down from the nursery, and Mrs. Fenelby brought him in, limp and sleeping, and sat with him in her arms. Mr. Fenelby explained why the meeting was called.

"It is because Laura and I are tired of this tariff nonsense," he explained. "You and Kitty have seen how it workseverybody in the house mad at one another"

"Not Billy and I," interposed Kitty. "Are we Billy?"

"Let us, for the sake of argument, suppose we are," said Billy. "We must give Tom a fair chance. It is his tariff, not ours."

"Very well," said Kitty; "we are all angry! Let us quarrel!"

"Seriously, now," said Mr. Fenelby, very seriously indeed, "this has got to stop! You and Kitty may think it is all a joke, but Laura and I went into this thing before you came, and we meant it seriously. We went into it in parliamentary form, and in good faith. Now we see it was all a mistake and we want to do away with it. If you will just take it seriously for five minutesif you can be sensible that longwe will not trouble you with it any more. Laura, awaken Bobberts!"

Mrs. Fenelby awakened the Territory by gently kissing him on his eyes, and he opened them and blinked sleepily at the ceiling.

"Congress is in session," said Mr. Fenelby. "And Laura moves that the Fenelby Domestic Tariff be repealed and annulled. I second it. All in favor of the motion say"

"Stop!" exclaimed Billy, rising from his chair. "I object to this! Kitty and I did not come in here to have such an important motion rushed through without consideration. It is not parliamentary. I want to make a speech."

"Oh, don't!" pleaded Mrs. Fenelby. "Think how late it is, Billy."

"Mr. President and Ladies of Congress," said Billy unrelentingly; "we are asked to repeal our tariff laws, our beneficent laws, enacted to send Bobberts to college. We stand in the presence of two cruel parents who would take away from their only Territory its sole chanceas we were informedof securing an education. We are asked to do this merely because there has been some slight difficulty in collecting the tariff tax. I am ashamed to be a State in a commonwealth that can put forward such an excuse. I care not what others may do, but as for me I shall never cast my vote to rob that poor innocent," he pointed feelingly toward Bobberts, "to rob him of his future happiness! Never. You won't either, will you, Kitty?"

"I should think not!" exclaimed Kitty. "Poor little Bobberts!"

Mr. Fenelby moved the papers on his desk nervously. He was tempted to say something about smuggling, but he controlled himself, for it would not do to antagonize onehalf of congress. He felt that Kitty and Billy had been planning some great feats of smuggling, and that they had no desire to have their fun spoiled by the repeal of the tariff. Probably no smugglers are free traders at heartfree trade would ruin their business.

He put the motion, and the vote was what he had expectedtwo for and two against the motion. It was not carried. For a few minutes all sat in silence, the air tingling with suppressed irritability. A word would have condensed it into cruel speech. It was Billy who broke the spell.

"I'm going out to smoke another dutypaid cigar before I turn in," he said. "Do you want to have a turn on the porch, Kitty?"

"I think not. I'm tired. I'll go up, I think," said Kitty, and they left the room together.

Mr. Fenelby gathered his papers and his book together and pushed them wearily into the desk. Then he dropped into a chair and looked sadly at the floor.

"Tom," said Laura, "can't we stop the tariff anyway?"

"Oh, no!" said her husband disconsolately. "We can't do anything. We've got to go ahead with the foolishness until Kitty and Billy go. They would laugh at us and crow over us all their lives if we didn't. Especially after the fool I have made of myself with this voting nonsense," he added bitterly.

Mrs. Fenelby sighed.

XI

THE COUP D'ÉTAT

The next morning dawned gloomily. The sky was a dull gray, and a sickening drizzle was falling, mixed with a thick fog that made everything and everybody soggy and damp. It was a most dismal and disheartening Sunday, without a ray of cheerfulness in it, and Mr. and Mrs. Fenelby felt the burden of the day keenly. The house had the usual Sunday morning air of untidiness. It was a bad day on which to take up the load of the tariff and carry it through twelve hours of servantless housekeeping.

Breakfast was a sad affair. Kitty and Billy, who seemed in high spirits, tried to give the meal an air of gaiety, but Mr. Fenelby was glum and his wife naturally reflected some of his feeling, and after a few attempts to liven things Kitty and Billy turned their attention to each other and left the Fenelbys alone with their gloom. As soon as breakfast was over, Kitty, after a weak suggestion that she should help Laura with the dishes, carried Billy away, saying that no matter what happened she was going to church. The Fenelbys were glad to have them go, and Mr. Fenelby helped Laura carry out the breakfast things.

"Laura," said Mr. Fenelby, "I lay awake a long time last night thinking about the tariff, and something has got to be done about it! I cannot, as the father of Bobberts, let it go on as it is going."

"I lay awake too," said Laura, "and I think exactly as you do, Tom."

"I knew you would," said Mr. Fenelby. "The way Kitty and Billy are acting is not to be borne. They acted last night as if you and I were not capable of raising our own child! I really cannot put another cent in that bank under the tariff law, Laura. Just think how it lookswe are not to be trusted to provide Bobberts with an education; we are not fit to decide how to raise the money for him. No, Kitty and Billy are to be his guardians. They don't trust us; they insist that we shall keep ourselves bound by the tariff system. They think we don't love dear little Bobberts, and they think they can make us provide for him, just because they have the balance of power!"

"Yes," said Laura sympathetically. "I thought of all that, Tom, and I don't think it does them much credit. It is easy enough for them to say there must be a tariff, when they bring hardly anything into the house that they have to pay duty on, but we have to keep the house going. We have to have vegetables and meat and all sorts of things, and they are making us pay duty, while all they have to do is to eat and have a good time. Bobberts is our child, Tom, and it ought to be for us to say what we will save for him, and how we will save it."

"That is just what I think," said Mr. Fenelby feelingly, "and I am not going to stand it any longer. I am going to have another meeting of congress this afternoon"

"They will vote just the same way," said Laura, hopelessly.

"Probably," said Mr. Fenelby. "But if they do we will end the whole thing."

"We can't send them away," said Laura. "We couldn't be so rude as that."

"No," said Mr. Fenelby, "but we will secede. You and I and Bobberts will secede from the Union. I never believed in secession, Laura, but I see now that there are times when conditions become so intolerable that there is nothing else to do. We will give them a chance to vote the tariff out of existence, and if they don't we will just secede from the Commonwealth of Bobberts. We will have a free trade commonwealth of our own, and Kitty and Billy can do as they please."

"Tom," said Mrs. Fenelby, "that is just what we will do!" And so it was settled.

By the time Kitty and Billy returned loiteringly from church Mr. Fenelby had progressed pretty well through four of the sixteen sections of the Sunday paper, and Mrs. Fenelby had Bobberts washed and dressed and was in the kitchen preparing dinner, which on Sunday was supposed to be at noon, but which, this Sunday, threatened to be about two o'clock. Kitty threw off her hat and dropped her umbrella in the hall and rushed for the kitchen. Billy merely glanced into the parlor, and seeing Tom holding the grim funny page uncompromisingly before his face, strolled out to the hammock.

"Laura," cried Kitty, "you must let me help you! And what do you think? We met Doctor Stafford, and he did prescribe whisky and rock candy for Bridget's cold! So I fixed everything all right. I rushed Billy around to Bridget's sister's and Bridget is just getting over her cold, so she was glad to come back to you. She says she never, never drinks except under her doctor's orders, and she said that if you hadn't been so hasty"

Mrs. Fenelby dropped the potato she was slicing. Her pretty mouth hardened.

"Kitty!" she exclaimed. "Now I shall never forgive you! I will never have Bridget in this kitchen again! It wasn't only that she drank, it was her awful, awful deceitfulness. It was that, Kitty, more than anything else. I won't have people about me who will not live up to the tariff poor dear Tom worked and worried to make! You may smuggle, Kitty, if you must be so low, and I certainly have no control over Billy, but my servants must not break the rules of this house. If that Bridget dares to put her head inside of this door I will send her about her business."

"Laura," said Kitty, "I wish you would be reasonablelike Billy and me. We talked it all over on the way to church, and we saw that it was Tom's crazy old tariff that was making all the trouble and driving Bridget away and everything, and we decided we would stop the tariff right away."

Laura's chin went into the air and her eyes flashed.

"You will stop the tariff!" she cried, turning red. "What right have you to stop anything in this house, Kitty? And it isn't a crazy tariff. It was a splendid idea, and no one but Tom would ever have thought of it, and it worked all right until you and Billy began spoiling it!"

"But I thought you wanted it stopped," said Kitty.

"I don't!" exclaimed Laura, bursting into tears. "It is a nice, lovely tariff, and if I ever said I didn't want it, it was because you aggravated me. I won't have it stopped. I won't be so mean to anything dear old Tom starts. It's Bobberts' tariff. You ought to think more of Bobberts than to suggest such a thing, if you don't love me."

Kitty stood back and looked at Laura as at some one possessed of evil spirits. Then she turned to the table and took up the potato knife and began slicing potatoes calmly.

"Very well, Laura," she said. "I tried to do what I thought you would like, but if you want the tariff so badly I shall certainly not oppose you. Hereafter, no matter what happens, Billy and I will vote for the tariff!"

"And Tom and I certainly will," said Laura between sobs. "We don't care who the tariff bothers, or how much trouble it is. We are always, always going to have a tarifffor ever and ever!"

When she told Mr. Fenelby this he was not as happy about it as might have been expected. He agreed that under the circumstances there was nothing else to do; that the tariff must become a permanent fixture; but he did not say so joyfully. He had more the air of a Job admitting that a continued succession of boils was inevitable. Job, under those circumstances was probably as placid as could be expected, but not hilarious, and neither was Mr. Fenelby.

Dinner was as gloomy as breakfast had been. It developed into one of the platestudying kind, with each of the four eating hastily and silently. Even Bobberts was not cheerful. He did not "coo" as usual, but stared unsmilingly at the ceiling. Into such a condition does a nation come when it suffers under a tax that is obnoxious, but which it cannot and will not repeal. When a nation gets into that condition one State can hardly ask another State to pass the butter, and when it does ask, its parliamentary courtesy is something frigidly polite. Suddenly Mrs. Fenelby looked up.

"Tom," she said, "there is somebody in the kitchen!"

Mr. Fenelby laid his fork softly on his plate and listened. There was no doubt of it. Someone was in the kitchen, gathering up the silverware. Mr. Fenelby arose and went into the kitchen. Almost immediately he returned. He returned because he either had to follow Bridget into the dining room or stay in the kitchen alone.

"It's me, ma'am," said Bridget. She planted herself before Mrs. Fenelby and placed her hands on her hips. Mrs. Fenelby arose. "I've come back," said Bridget.

"And you can go again," said Mrs. Fenelby regally. "I do not want you, you can go!"

"Yes, ma'am," said Bridget. "'Tis all th' same t' mestay or go, ma'am,but I'll be askin' ye t' pay me a month's wages, Mrs. Fenelby, if ye want me t' go. A month's wages or a month's noticethat is th' law, ma'am."

"The idea!" exclaimed Mrs. Fenelby. "I have not even hired you, yet!"

"No, ma'am," said Bridget, "but th' young lady has. She hired me with her own mouth, at me own sister Maggie's, who will be witness t' it, an' I have been workin' in th' kitchen already. I've washed th' spoons."

"The young lady," said Mrs. Fenelby coldly, "has no right to hire servants for me."

"And hasn't she, ma'am?" said Bridget angrily. "Let th' judge in th' courthouse say if she has or hasn't! Don't try t' fool me, Missus Fenelby, ma'am. I've worked here before, ma'am, an' I know all about th' Commonwealth way ye have of doin' things. Wan of ye has as good a right t' vote me into a job as another has, Mrs. Fenelby, an' th' young lady an' th' young gintleman both asked me t' come. Even a poor ign'rant Irish girl has rights, Mrs. Fenelby, an' hired I was, t' worrk for th' Commonwealth. An' here I stay, without ye choose t' hand me me month's wages!"

Mrs. Fenelby looked appealingly at Tom, and Tom looked at Billy.

"I think she'd win, if she took it to law," said Billy. "You know how the judges are. And if she brought up the matter of the Commonwealth, you know you did make Kitty and me full partakers in it."

"Tom," said Mrs. Fenelby, "pay her a month's wages and let her go!"

Mr. Fenelby moved uneasily. He had put all his money into Bobberts' bank. In all the house there was not a month's wages except in Bobberts' bank. Mr. Fenelby looked toward the bank.

"Never!" said Billy. "I put money into that, and so did Kitty. It is for Bobberts, not for month's wages. I object."

Mr. Fenelby looked away from the bank. He looked, helplessly, all around the room, and ended by looking at Laura.

"My dear," he said, "I think we had better keep Bridget."

"I think ye had!" said Bridget. "For there ain't no way t' git rid of me. I'm here, ma'am, an' I don't bear no ill will. I forgive ye all, an' I'm willin' t' let bygones be bygones, excipt one or two things, which ye will have t' change."

"The idea!" exclaimed Mrs. Fenelby. Bridget shrugged her shoulders.

"Have it yer own way, ma'am," she said. "I am not one that would dictate t' th' lady of th' house. I am no dictator, ma'am, an' I don't wish t' be, but here I am an' here I stay, an' 'tis no fault of mine if some things riles me temper and makes me act as I shouldn't. I'm one that likes things t' be peaceful, ma'am, for no one knows how much row a girrl can make in th' house better 'n than I does, especially when she's hired by th' month an' can't be fired. I can't forget one Mrs. Grasset I worked for, ma'am, an' her that miserable an' cryin' all th' time, just because I had one of me bad timper spells. I should hate t' have one of thim here, Mrs. Fenelby."

"Well," said Mr. Fenelby, controlling his righteous indignation as best he could, "what is it you want?"

"I want no more of thim tariff doin's!" said Bridget firmly. "Thim tariff doin's is more than mortal mind can stand, Mr. Fenelby, sir! Nawthin' I ever had t' do with in anny of me places riled me up like thim tariff doin's, an' we will have no more tariff in th' house, if ye please, sir."

"Well, of all the impert" began Mr. Fenelby angrily, but Mrs. Fenelby put her hand on his arm and quieted him.

"Tom," she said, "please be careful! You do not have to spend your days with Bridget, and I do! Don't be rash. Send her into the kitchen until we talk it over."

Bridget went, willingly. She gathered an armful of dishes, and went into her throneroom, bearing her head high. She felt that she was master and she was.

"Now, this Commonwealth" began Mr. Fenelby, when the kitchen door had closed, but Billy stopped him.

"Stop being foolish, Tom," he said. "What Commonwealth are you talking about? This is not a Commonwealththis is an unlimited dictatorship, and Bridget is sole dictator! Wake up; don't you know a coup d'état when you see one? Can't you tell a usurper by sight?"

Mr. Fenelby looked moodily at the kitchen door.

"That is what it is," said Billy decidedly. "The dictator has smashed your republic under her iron heel; your laws are all back numbersif she wants any laws, she will let you know. I know the signs. When a Great One rises up in the midst of a Republic and puts her hands on her hips and says 'What are you going to do about it?' and there isn't anything to do about it, you have a dictator, and all that you can do is knuckle down and be good."

There was a minute's silence. The Commonwealth was dying hard.

"I could shake the money out of Bobberts' bank," said Mr. Fenelby, but even as he said it Bobberts wailed. His voice arose clear and strong in protest against that or against something else. The kitchen door swung open and the Dictator ran in and approached the Heir, and Bobberts held out his arms.

"Bless th' darlin'," said Bridget, cuddling him in her arms, but Mrs. Fenelby frowned.

"Give him to me," she said sternly, and Bridget turned to her. And then, in the eyes of all the Commonwealth, Bobberts turned his back on his own mother and clung to the Dictator! Clung, and squealed, until the danger of separation was over.

"You see!" said Billy, triumphantly.

Mrs. Fenelby sighed. The Dictator had won. The tariff was dead.

"And in our house," said Kitty, cheerfully, "we won't have any tariff, will we, Billy?"

"Your house!" exclaimed Mrs. Fenelby, forgetting all about the Dictator in the new interest, and brightening into herself again.

"Our house," said Kitty proudly. "Mine and Billy's."

"Our house," echoed Billy, blushing. "We can't stand a Dictator, and we are going to secede andand have a United State of our own."

"Isn't it splendid about Kitty and Billy?" said Mrs. Fenelby that evening to Tom, as they bent over Bobberts' crib. "And if it hadn't been for our tariff driving them together I don't believe it would ever have happened."

"It's fine!" said Mr. Fenelby. "Fine! And that other set of Eugene Field will do for a wedding present!"

THE END